Escape
to the
River
Sea

Escape to the River Sea

Emma Carroll

INSPIRED BY THE WORLD OF
EVA IBBOTSON

Published 2022 by Macmillan Children's Books
an imprint of Pan Macmillan
The Smithson, 6 Briset Street, London EC1M 5NR
EU representative: Macmillan Publishers Ireland Ltd, 1st Floor,
The Liffey Trust Centre, 117–126 Sheriff Street Upper
Dublin 1, D01 YC43
Associated companies throughout the world
www.panmacmillan.com

ISBN 978-1-5290-6270-0

5 7 9 8 6

A CIP catalogue record for this book is available from the British Library.

Printed and bound by CPI Group (UK) Ltd, Croydon CR0 4YY

To my dearest dad,
who taught me one pudding is never enough.

Chapter One

Rosa Sweetman hated goodbyes. In her short eleven-year-old life, and though she'd had more than her fair share of them, two had been particularly agonizing. The first, years ago, was when she'd hugged her mother and older sister, Liesel, goodbye on a dark, rain-blown station platform in Vienna. The other, just last month, had been at the gates of Westwood, waving off the twenty schoolgirls who'd shared her bedroom with their late-night gossip through the bleak years of war.

She'd been lucky – all the girls had – to spend the war safe from enemy bombs here at Westwood, the rambling country home of a dimple-chinned Englishman called Sir Clovis, who'd suddenly found himself doing his bit for the war effort by taking in evacuees. Rosa had been the first, rescued from another station platform – this time Euston Station, in London. As fate would have it, Sir Clovis missed his train, and the person supposed to be collecting Rosa was struck down with TB. So, when he'd seen one little girl left behind and the harried volunteers wondering what to do with her, Sir Clovis offered her a home at Westwood.

The house itself was a vast, ugly brute of a place, draughty and mouldering, with battlements like rows of untidy teeth. There'd been no other children, or animals, here when Rosa arrived, just long, echoing corridors, and too many unused rooms. A few months later, war broke out and when the schoolgirls were evacuated from their city homes, she was very glad: filling Westwood with children certainly improved it.

It hadn't stopped with children. One night, the local zoo was hit by German bombs. Since there were enough hazards during wartime without wild animals roaming the streets, it was decided the creatures must be shot, or evacuated. Within days, Westwood's stables and paddocks, where the previous owner had kept horses, became home to two ostriches, a dozen snakes, five zebras, ten meerkats and a beautiful jaguar named Opal.

Then one calm June day, peace was declared, and everything changed again. There was no longer any reason for the children or zoo animals to be at Westwood. It was safe to go home. Despite the cheering, fireworks and the celebration bonfire up on Westwood Moor, all Rosa could think of was being the only child again, rattling around Westwood all by herself.

Her mother had promised she'd come for her.

'We'll be on the next train out of Vienna, right behind you,' she'd sworn that night at the station.

Yet seven years and a world war later, Rosa was still waiting.

She'd not received so much as a letter in all that time. Sometimes, she felt she was forgetting Vienna because her old life existed only as smells or sounds – apple cake baking, hoofbeats on cobbles. It worried her, too, that her own mother and sister wouldn't recognize her. She'd grown a lot in seven years: longer legs, freckles, hair a darker shade of brown. But Rosa's nature was a hopeful one – that hadn't changed. She told herself to be patient, even if Westwood seemed to be emptying quicker than water from a bathtub.

As it turned out, work repairing the city's zoo took longer than anticipated. It was the following February before the animals finally went home. On the morning the zoo trucks were due to arrive, Rosa awoke to a noise like distant thunder. Out on the landing, the grandfather clock chimed seven, though it always ran ten minutes slow. The rumbling was getting louder. Rosa sat up, listening: the sound was of vehicles coming down the lane.

Throwing off the bedclothes, Rosa grabbed her blouse, cardigan and skirt off the bedroom chair, and stuffed her feet in her shoes. She hadn't expected the zoo this early. She'd hoped to give Opal the jaguar one last breakfast, and running down the stairs, hair uncombed, cardigan unbuttoned, she didn't feel ready to say goodbye.

When the zoo had first arrived, she begged the zookeeper's son, Billy, to let her look after Opal. She'd had a kitten back in Vienna, the same black-brown colour, and the lack of pets here at Westwood was another thing Rosa had never got used to.

'If you want her to like you, then feed her pilchards,' Billy advised as they watched Opal inspect the corners of the stable that was to be her new home. 'She's not really black, d'you see?' He pointed to the animal's flank, which, when the light caught it, was a rich, rusty brown, the jaguar spots dark splodges in her coat.

Rosa didn't know much about jaguars – and what she did, she'd hastily read about while balanced on a chair in Westwood's library. But it was important to her not to let Billy – or Opal – down. Billy was the one person who *had* written to her regularly during the war, mostly to give advice on his precious jaguar.

Opal's eaten two rabbits and given herself the hiccups . . . Rosa wrote once, to which Billy replied, *Try rubbing her tummy. Or give her warmed milk . . .* She followed his instructions diligently. *It worked! She's purring!*

Writing to Billy made Rosa feel, though they'd only met in person once, as if they were friends. He was older than her, with curly blond hair and dirty fingernails, and – she secretly suspected – enjoyed knowing things that she didn't. Not that Rosa minded: learning about jaguars had been a joy.

Today, though, it was time for another round of goodbyes.

'Careful!'

Rosa skidded to a halt on the landing, narrowly avoiding Westwood's only housemaid, Minnie. The door to the biggest front bedroom was propped open with

Minnie's cleaning box. Her arms were full of fresh bed-linen. Though she had an uncanny knack for looking busy even when she wasn't, today Minnie seemed genuinely rushed off her feet.

'Sorry, Minnie. I was miles away,' Rosa admitted.

'No change there.' Minnie tutted, shouldering past. 'Master wants this room ready for tonight, when I've enough to do already. Oh, and you've missed breakfast, so don't go begging scraps from Mrs Barnes, neither.'

Rosa flushed guiltily. With pilchards in short supply and meat on the ration, she'd often had to pester Westwood's cook for Opal's food, which wasn't the done thing in wartime.

'Who's coming to stay?' Rosa asked.

'Be blowed if I know,' Minnie replied. 'Though it's someone they weren't expecting. It's all been a bit of a rush.'

Out in the lane, a horn beeped.

'The zoo's here!' Rosa cried.

With a shriek, they both ran into the bedroom and straight to the big bay window that overlooked the drive. Coming through the gates, emerging from under the winter trees, the first vehicle appeared. Behind it were more trucks, some large, canvas-covered army-types, others smaller, the size of a grocer's van. The convoy came to a halt at the front of the house where, in olden days, carriages would've turned. There, they were greeted, as all Westwood visitors were, by a bizarre headless statue of Hercules wrestling a snake.

Truck doors opened, voices calling between the vehicles.

'Load the birds and reptiles first. Leave the big animals till last,' ordered a ruddy-faced man who Rosa recognized as Mr Macintyre, the zoo owner and Billy's dad.

The driveway was suddenly swarming with people in overalls, caps, boots and protective gloves. None of them seemed to be Billy. Mr Macintyre unbolted the sides of the trucks. Boxes, wicker crates, ropes and headcollars were unloaded and whisked away.

Minnie gave her apron a quick smooth. 'I'd best go down. That front door won't open itself.'

From the drawing room across the landing came the rustle of newspapers being folded.

'Well, dearest, I believe they're here,' announced Westwood's dimple-chinned owner to his wife, Lady Prue.

Sir Clovis had once been a stage actor: this was still evident in his upright posture and fondness for eye-catching clothes. Though his real name was Finn Taverner, for some inexplicable reason everyone called him Sir Clovis. Like the stodgy dinners and scratchy tweed clothes she'd had to endure at Westwood, there was much about life in England that Rosa didn't understand. And this was despite being half-English herself.

'Righty-ho!' Lady Prue clapped her hands briskly and came out onto the landing. 'Action stations, everyone!'

At the bay window, Rosa was still trying to spot Billy. She couldn't bear it if he wasn't here. She'd been so eager to see him reunited with Opal. It was the one thing that might take the sting out of saying goodbye.

A boy darted about from behind one of the trucks, so quickly she almost missed him. Then one of the men called out, 'Oi, where's that lad off to?' The boy kept running, before disappearing round the side of the house. Rosa grinned.

It *was* Billy.

The curly blond hair was the giveaway. And the fact he was making a beeline for the stable yard, where the jaguar was kept. Rushing downstairs to join him, Rosa was almost at the back door when a yell from the hallway made her stop.

'OUTER GARMENTS!' boomed Lady Prue, who, despite being as strong as a shire horse, swore by the practicalities of a good tweed coat.

Reluctantly, Rosa went back for hers, a horrid, itchy green thing with leather buttons and a belted waist. There was no point in resisting: no one ever argued with Lady Prue and won.

Outside, though the morning itself was damp and unremarkable, the air crackled with noise. At the front of the house, it was human voices, at the rear, hissing ostriches, chattering meerkats, the stamp and snort of impatient zebras. Rosa ran all the way to the stable yard. She found Billy, his back to her, unbolting Opal's stable door. All over again it hit her that this jaguar she'd got up every morning to feed was going home. Everything was leaving Westwood: everything but her. To her added frustration, her nose was now tingling in the way it did when she was about to burst into tears. She was grateful Billy hadn't yet realized she was there.

She watched, fascinated, as he opened the door – not cautiously like she did, but pushing it wide open. Moving casually, whistling, he placed a pile of ropes just inside. Something moved in the darkness. A pair of green-gold eyes blinked. A pink mouth opened. Realizing it was Billy, Opal rushed towards him in one fluid movement.

'Hey there, big cat,' Billy murmured as she stood up, paws on his shoulders as if hugging him.

Opal covered his cheeks, his hair, his ears with big, rough licks.

'She's so pleased to see you!' cried Rosa, who was now definitely on the verge of tears.

Billy turned his head, grinning. 'Hullo! I wondered when you'd show up!'

He looked different from how she remembered – taller, older. The jaguar's licking had made his fringe stand on end.

'You've done a fine job, keeping her so tip-top,' Billy remarked.

Rosa blushed with pride. 'Thanks. I loved doing it.'

'It's hard work, though, isn't it?'

'You did give me lots of advice,' she reminded him.

Billy beckoned her into the stable. 'Want to come and say your goodbyes?'

Once inside, Rosa pulled the stable door behind her.

Taking a deep breath, telling herself not to ruin it by crying, she reached towards the jaguar.

'Goodbye, beautiful cat,' she murmured.

Opal sniffed her hand briefly, then yawned. She was more interested in Billy, that was obvious, and though it hurt a little to be cast off so quickly, Rosa was glad. It felt right for them to be together – the cat rubbing her head against Billy's hair, purring like an engine.

'You in there, lad?' a man shouted from the yard. 'Running off like that when there's work to do!'

In the dim light of the stable, Rosa saw the joy draining from Billy's face.

'Yup, I'm here!' he called in reply.

'Then bring her out and stop wasting time!' the man answered.

'That's my pa, on to me as usual.' Billy sighed.

'He sounds a bit fierce,' remarked Rosa.

Billy scowled, suddenly defensive. 'Why, what's yours like?'

'I dunno,' she admitted. All she did know was that he'd left Vienna just after she was born, though no one had ever told her why, or what had happened to him.

Just as Billy went to say something, Mr Macintyre roared: 'GET A MOVE ON!'

It made them jump. Billy grabbed the pile of ropes he'd left by the door.

'What d'you want me to do?' Rosa asked, wanting to help if she could.

'Watch her,' he warned, because Opal's mood had changed.

She was sniffing the air, ears flicking and swivelling. The purring had stopped. The end of her tail thump-thumped against the straw. It wasn't a good sign.

'She's smelled the trucks,' Billy said, not taking his eyes off the cat. 'She's not a good traveller, this one.'

Rosa reckoned it had more to do with Billy's dad's temper, but kept quiet. It wasn't her business any more.

The cat swung away from them and began pacing the stable. With some difficulty, Billy got a rope round Opal's shoulders, murmuring, 'Easy girl, easy now,' which seemed to work. Apart from the tip of her tail, the cat grew still again.

'Phew!' Billy grimaced. 'That was a bit—'

In a sudden leap, Opal lunged for the door. The force knocked Rosa against the wall. Billy yelped, the rope slipping from his hands. The door was shut and bolted – at least, Rosa assumed it was, and she'd been the last person in. She realized now the door was slightly ajar. She hadn't secured the bolt properly. It was enough, Rosa saw in horror, for Opal to push it open, which she did in one swift movement. The cat slipped through the door and was gone.

Out in the yard, Billy's father cursed. They found him, hands on his head, clenching fistfuls of his own hair.

'What are you playing at, lad?' he cried. 'Get after her, quick!'

They were already too late. Fifty yards away at the

paddock fence, Opal crouched, ready to spring.

'Hurry! She's going to—' Rosa cried.

Jump.

In a smooth, fluid arc, Opal was over the fence.

Billy and his father, frantically trying to untangle more ropes, missed it. The ostriches sidestepped crossly, their wings stuck out like elbows. Ignoring them, Opal ran across the grass towards the distant tree-line. Rosa knew she should tell them the direction in which the cat had gone. But she couldn't bring herself to, because it looked so easy, so hopeful, the way Opal had left Westwood behind.

Chapter Two

When he realized, Mr Macintyre exploded.

'You ruddy idiot!' he screamed at Billy. 'Don't you know how much that animal's worth?'

Clearly Billy did because he'd gone very pale.

Mr Macintyre turned to Rosa. 'And what were you doing, standing there like a lemon?'

'I . . . ummm.' She was alarmed by the vein throbbing in his forehead like a very fat earthworm. He was so angry it felt pointless trying to explain.

It was her fault, she knew, for not bolting the door. All this time she'd tried so hard to look after Opal properly, and she'd almost managed it – hadn't Billy told her so? But a moment's slip-up and now she'd ruined everything.

'That jaguar won't last five minutes out there!' Mr Macintyre fumed, waving at the fields beyond Westwood, which were dotted with grazing cows and sheep. 'The second she goes near anyone's livestock they'll shoot her on sight.'

Rosa glanced at Billy, startled: *shoot* her?

Billy wiped an arm across his eyes: he was crying.

'Please stop,' Rosa begged him, feeling totally and utterly miserable.

He did, though only because a small woman with radish-red cheeks was now yelling over the fence.

'There's a creature hiding in the hedge. It's scaring my ewes.' The woman was Mrs Penwick, who rented one of Westwood's farms. 'If it's yours, you'd better claim it fast, before I take my rifle to it.'

Rosa groaned. The animal had to be Opal.

'What did I tell you?' Mr Macintyre cried, head in hands again. 'Not *even* five minutes on the loose, and here we are!'

'Don't shoot her! There's been a misunderstanding!' pleaded Rosa.

There was a click as the yard gate opened.

'A misunderstanding, eh?' remarked Sir Clovis.

Everyone turned to see Westwood's owner striding towards them in his best tweeds and finest brogues. He looked every inch the country gent, despite having never ridden a horse or walked a dog in all the time Rosa had lived here.

'It'll be all right now,' Rosa whispered to Billy.

Sir Clovis was good at fixing tricky situations. There was a charm to him that quickly put other grown-ups at ease. It'd certainly helped at Euston Station all those years ago.

'Perhaps one of you good people could tell me what's going on?' Sir Clovis asked, rubbing his hands like he meant business.

It had an effect on Mr Macintyre, who, at last, managed to explain the situation without raising his voice.

'—so we've got to catch her,' Mr Macintyre finished. 'She's our star attraction, what everyone comes to see. A taste of the Amazon in our humble zoo.'

Sir Clovis gave the zookeeper's shoulder an affable pat.

'We'll find her in no time,' Sir Clovis assured him in his best stage voice that had once filled theatres around the globe. And to Mrs Penwick: 'My sincerest apologies. I can't imagine how this could've happened.'

Rosa stared at the ground.

It was all her fault: she knew it, Billy knew it. Sir Clovis too, she sensed, realized it was her fault. In leaving their animals here, the zoo had trusted him to keep them safe. And the one thing Sir Clovis despised was putting on a bad show. If there'd been a dog here now, he'd have shouted at it, but there wasn't, so he turned on Rosa.

'Well, don't just stand there, child! Let's find this beast!'

While the adults searched the nearby fields and wood, Rosa checked the lane that led from Westwood to the village. Apart from today's zoo trucks, few vehicles ever came down it – the grocer's van on a Tuesday, the postman once a day on his bicycle – so it was the sort of quiet spot Opal might be drawn to.

Rosa insisted Billy come with her. If they found his jaguar together, there was a slim possibility they might come out of this still friends. Billy hadn't spoken a word to her since Opal had gone. When she thought of how much she'd wanted to see him again – and how thrilled he'd been to see Opal – it made everything worse.

'Ugh, it's a swamp,' groaned Billy, as they set off down the lane.

The zoo's trucks had gouged huge ruts into the mud, spraying the hedges brown on either side. It looked more like a ploughed field than a road.

'Keep your eyes peeled for pawprints,' Rosa said with forced cheerfulness.

In fact, the mud was like soup. It clung to everything. Billy, at least, wore boots with a sensible grip. But Rosa's stout walking shoes – purchased for her at the same time as the awful tweed coat – made a revolting slurping noise with every step.

When they reached the village, Rosa wondered if they should put a card in the post-office window, or knock on doors in the way people did when they'd lost a cat. Or they could ask at the tea shop where Mrs Barnes the cook used to work. The trouble with telling people, though, was it panicked them. There'd been a story once about a zebra escaping London Zoo during the Blitz. It'd taken three days and police marksmen to recapture the animal. The last thing they needed right now was more people with guns.

Anyway, Billy said they should turn back.

'She's not been this way – it's obvious.' He sighed.

'How?' Rosa wanted to know. 'Have you seen any clues? Are you tracking her like you're in the jungle?'

Billy snorted. 'Don't be daft. All I know is she wouldn't want to get her feet wet in the mud.'

Rosa wasn't sure this was true. She'd read that jaguars were strong swimmers and liked water, though it probably wasn't the right time to say so.

'Why would she run away from *me* of all people?' Billy asked, close to tears again.

'She *was* pleased to see you,' Rosa agreed.

Opal had looked even more pleased to be galloping away across the paddock, but she thought it best not to mention that, either.

By the end of the morning, every field, copse, outbuilding and lane local to Westwood had been scoured. But, after the initial sighting under Mrs Penwick's hedge, the jaguar had vanished into thin air. No one knew what to do next. Rosa's eyes were annoyingly prickly again. The search parties, having returned to the stable yard, were fed up and hungry. Sir Clovis's assurances were starting to wear thin.

'I should've known this would happen,' Mr Macintyre muttered through gritted teeth. 'Letting amateurs take care of our animals.'

'We'll keep searching,' Sir Clovis promised. 'All day and night, if we have to.' Though Rosa knew all too well what would happen when the lunch gong sounded. Not even a missing jaguar could keep Sir Clovis from his food.

Mealtimes at Westbrook were legendary: the roast meat, the cream sauces and custard pies, the five-course suppers, the never-ending cake. Rationing hadn't dented the scope of Mrs Barnes's menus. There'd been much moving of buttons on waistbands by the time the schoolgirl evacuees had gone home.

'You'll see things differently after lunch. I'm sure of it,' Sir Clovis insisted.

'We've no time for *lunch*!' Mr Macintyre's colour was rising again. 'That animal cost money! The lost ticket sales to the zoo *cost money*. It's time we talked compensation. A chap like you, with this big house, should be able to put his hand in his pocket.'

For the first time, Sir Clovis looked nervous.

In reality, there was little spare money at Westwood. The roof leaked and there was mould around the window frames. You only had to glimpse the west wing of the house to see it was pretty much falling down. There'd been talk, recently, of selling off some of the farmland to raise extra funds, which had led to a flurry of letters arriving. Rosa, who kept an eagle eye on such things, noticed some of these – bizarrely – bore a Brazilian postmark.

'There must be somewhere we haven't looked yet!' Rosa pleaded.

Mr Macintyre shook his head. 'I've not got time for this. You'll be hearing from me, Clovis – in writing. Official, like.'

Yelling at his zoo staff to load the remaining animals into the trucks, he stormed out of the yard. There was a second when a bewildered Billy caught Rosa's eye. She would've done anything, right then, to make things better.

'I'm sorry,' she said, for the hundredth time.

But even to her own ears the words sounded hollow: what could possibly make up for losing a jaguar?

She watched, lump in throat, as Billy disappeared round the corner. This wasn't the sort of goodbye for which she'd been bracing herself: this was ten times worse.

From the front of the house came the sound of raised voices again, the crunch of feet – and hooves – on gravel, the thudding of tailgates being raised as the trucks made ready to leave.

Moments later, as predicted, the lunch gong sounded.

'I'm not hungry,' Rosa said when Sir Clovis tried to hurry her indoors.

For once, instead of insisting she eat lunch, he seemed to understand, and asked her to take a message to Westwood's chauffeur. 'Tell Jarvis to ready the motor car. Our guest is arriving on the two o'clock train.'

After the agony of watching the zoo trucks depart, Rosa set off down the drive to the gatehouse where old Mr Jarvis lived. He'd been at Westwood ever since the time there *were* grand gates to open and shut, and visitors arrived unannounced in carriages, rather than simply telephoning ahead. Unlike Minnie, Rosa also got the sense he quite liked her.

Feeling wretched, she barely gave much thought to who the person coming on the train might be. Generally, Westwood wasn't the sort of house you visited for fun: the grim look of the place was enough to put most people off.

In all the years she'd lived here, Rosa had rarely seen any visitors come and go. Sir Clovis and Lady Prue tended to keep themselves to themselves, and though they'd always been kind to Rosa and the schoolgirls, they weren't the types for hugging, or offering comforting chats. Still, the fact Minnie had cleaned what was probably the best bedroom in the house suggested someone important was coming to stay.

When Rosa arrived at the gatehouse, Mr Jarvis already knew about Opal. He opened the door with an almost-amused look on his face.

'What's all this nonsense, then, letting a big cat escape?' he asked, taking in her filthy socks and shoes.

Mr Jarvis often teased her affectionately, and she didn't mind at jot. But today it was the last straw. Rosa's chin wobbled. A big fat tear slid down her cheek.

'I didn't mean to let her go.' She sniffed.

'Here, now, don't you go upsetting yourself.' Mr Jarvis softened. 'Big cat like that, shut up in a stable. Was bound to happen sooner or later.'

'She did look incredible, running away,' admitted Rosa. 'I think maybe she didn't want to go back to the zoo.'

'Hmmm.' Mr Jarvis rubbed his jaw. 'Can't blame her, can you? Bet she'd rather take her chances up on Westwood Moor.'

'Westwood Moor?' Rosa hadn't considered this.

The moor lay about two miles from the estate. It was a desolate, windswept place, strewn with peat bogs, rocks and rust-coloured bracken. As a rule, Rosa didn't go there.

No one did, unless it was for a celebratory bonfire: it was too bleak and blustery for walking.

'Won't they search up there?' Rosa asked.

The idea amused Mr Jarvis. 'Ha! It'll be like looking for a needle in a haystack, that will.'

In her mind's eye, Rosa pictured Opal slinking away across the field, all sleek fur and muscle. Maybe, with a bit of luck and cunning, and if no one took a shot at her, she *could* survive in the wild. Rosa decided she'd write to Billy and tell him what Mr Jarvis had suggested, in the hope it might cheer him up.

'You're not here to talk jaguars, though, are you?' Mr Jarvis reminded her.

'Oh no, sorry.' Rosa rubbed her face dry. 'I've a message.'

She told him about leaving now to meet the two o'clock train.

'Ah! She's arriving earlier, then,' he said cryptically.

'Who is it?' Rosa asked.

'The lady coming from Europe.'

All the blood drained from Rosa's head. She swayed slightly.

'*Europe?*' she croaked. 'A lady? What's her name?'

'Well now, I didn't catch that part, what with my hearing not always being sharp.'

Hadn't Minnie told her that the visitor was someone they weren't expecting?

A warm, solid feeling filled Rosa's chest. She knew. She just *knew.* Who else would be coming here from Europe?

On a day when everything else had gone wrong, she felt as if her luck was changing. This visitor *had* to be her mother. Or her sister, Liesel. Finally, they were coming for her as they'd promised all those years ago. She'd no longer have to struggle to remember a long-ago goodbye. Her family would be here, hugging her hello. It was almost too much to be real. She just hoped she didn't die of excitement before two o'clock.

Chapter Three

Rosa followed Mr Jarvis to the garage where the Rolls-Royce was kept.

'Let me come with you to the station!' she begged.

The motor car itself was an immaculate silver grey that matched the chauffeur's jacket and silver-brimmed cap.

'In those shoes?' Mr Jarvis cast a horrified look at Rosa's filthy footwear.

She tore off her socks and shoes, flinging them aside. 'There! Ready!'

That still left the problem of her mud-splattered legs on the car's spotless upholstery, but the flare of hope in Rosa's face touched Mr Jarvis's old heart.

'Gah, go on, get in,' he relented.

The swamp-like lane took a fair bit of negotiating. But much revving and a few wheel spins later, they pulled into Westwood Halt station just as the church clock chimed two. The platform was reached by a flight of steep iron steps. Rosa bolted up them, leaving Mr Jarvis, with his bad knees, easing himself out of the car.

At the top of the steps, she was surprised to find the platform deserted. The stationmaster's ginger cat lay washing itself in a patch of sunshine. The stationmaster, still sitting in his little office, didn't look up from his newspaper. Overhead, the station clock ticked lazily past the hour: the train was late.

Rosa tried to be calm. But after waiting so long to see her mother – or Liesel – these final minutes felt like torture. Westwood Halt, being only a small station, had a ridiculously short platform, so there wasn't much room for anxious pacing in bare feet. She had to make do with chewing the end of her plait. The cat yawned; the clock ticked on.

After what felt like an age, the stationmaster emerged from his office. There was still no train in sight, yet just beyond the station a red signal flipped up. Rosa's plait-end fell from her mouth. She rushed to the edge of the platform, so excited she felt sick.

She heard the train before she saw it, huffing and sighing. Then the black, round-faced engine came nosing into view. She counted eight carriages on behind, which made it too long for the platform. It slid into the station in a cloud of steam. And moved right past her. For a second, Rosa panicked that it wasn't stopping at all. But, when the steam cleared, the brakes squealed one last time, and the train was still.

The engine itself was way down the track. Only the very end of the train was level with the platform. Any passengers in the front five carriages wanting to get off had to jump onto the bank. It was from one of these that a door opened. A woman, carrying a suitcase, stepped down onto the grass.

As Rosa rushed forward, the stationmaster grabbed her by the scruff of her coat.

'No trespassing on the track!' he barked, holding her back.

Though Rosa tried her hardest to squirm free, he held onto her until the woman reached the safety of the platform.

'Now you can say your hellos,' he said, finally letting her go.

Rosa didn't move. It was suddenly hard to breathe. This woman with the suitcase coming towards her wasn't her mother. Or her sister. She was small with dark-brown hair, wearing a navy skirt and jacket.

'Oh! But you're—' Rosa tried to say.

The woman stopped, glancing behind her.

'Were you expecting someone else?' she asked.

Rosa gulped. Nodded. The tingling behind her eyes started up again. Not wanting to cry in front of this stranger, she wiped her face roughly, and was glad that Mr Jarvis had now joined them on the platform.

'Ah, you must be—' he began.

'Dr Fielding,' the woman informed him. 'And you must be here from Westwood to collect me?'

Mr Jarvis assured her that he was, and went to take her luggage.

The woman insisted, very crisply, that she could carry her own suitcase, thank you. Rosa was too miserable to notice much else about her. Coat still bunched around her shoulders, her plait still damp at its end, she followed Dr Fielding and Mr Jarvis to the car.

Back at Westwood, Rosa went straight to her room. There, with the door closed, she flung herself onto her bed and sobbed into her pillow. To have her hopes raised then smashed to tiny pieces was more than she could bear. The war in Europe was over. People had gone home to their families.

So why was she still waiting for hers?

Every day, Rosa checked the post, then double-checked in case she'd missed an envelope in her mother's distinctive curly writing. But nothing ever arrived. Lady Prue, who read the newspapers avidly, said terrible things had happened in Europe during the war.

'Perhaps you could think of us as your family?' Sir Clovis had said to Rosa recently, as if he wasn't expecting her mother, either.

It was a kind offer, but they *weren't* her family, and no amount of thinking would change it. You only had to look at the Taverner family portraits hanging in Westwood's picture gallery. The Taverners were blonde, with expressive faces and winter-sky-blue eyes. Rosa Sweetman was brown-haired, brown-eyed, and had a mole at the tail end of her left eyebrow.

'Thank you,' she'd said, politely but firmly, 'but my mother *will* come for me. If you don't mind, I'll keep waiting.'

But the waiting grew more painful every day.

All this crying wasn't helping much, and when Rosa sat up to blow her nose the pillow crackled. She slid her hand underneath and pulled out the white card she kept there. These days, the document was crumpled and grubby-looking, mostly because, almost every night before putting her light out, Rosa would read the front and back of the card. It helped her to remember who she was.

On the front was a small photo of Rosa, aged three, staring very seriously at the camera. Her hair was shorter then, in bunches. Her mother must've cut her fringe because it sat high above her eyebrows and wasn't very straight. The picture was taken the night Rosa had left Vienna.

Her name, *Rosa Sweetman*, was handwritten under the photo, though time and damp fingers had smudged the ink, so she could just as easily have been *Rosa Sweeting* or *Rosa Sweetland*. Underneath this, the address of their apartment in Vienna was still legible.

A *Mrs Ethel Bellinger of St Albans, Hertfordshire* was mentioned, too. She was the sponsor who'd paid Rosa's fare from Vienna, and promised her a safe home here in England. But Mrs Bellinger had been too sick to collect her from Euston Station, in the end, which was how Rosa had ended up at Westwood.

The back of the card intrigued her even more. For here, in pencil, was a scribbled message from her mother. Rosa liked to think she'd written it in a rush as they'd waited for the train. The message was in the form of a short piece of music called: 'Stars of the Forest'. Though Rosa couldn't yet read music she cherished it: it was the only thing of her mother's she still had.

When bad dreams woke Rosa in the night, it was a real comfort, knowing her mother's writing was there, tucked under her pillow. Today, though, it didn't help at all. It was just another reminder – like the business with Opal had been – that being hopeful was a complete waste of time.

By evening, Rosa decided she'd cried enough. Having missed lunch, she was also ravenous. So, when the dinner gong sounded, she splashed cold water on her face, put on clean socks, wiped her shoes and went downstairs.

Already the grown-ups were deep in conversation at the dining-room table: Lady Prue in her favourite silk frock from her 'flapper girl' days, Sir Clovis in his best plum velvet cloak. Rosa hesitated in the doorway, realizing she'd forgotten to dress for dinner.

'It *is* rather rude inviting myself here like this. I do apologize,' Dr Fielding was saying.

She was partially hidden behind an enormous silver candelabra. Though the ground floor rooms at Westbrook had electricity, Sir Clovis insisted on candles at dinner which, if you didn't eat fast enough, tended to drip wax onto the food.

'I confess I've never clapped eyes on this notebook you speak of, but, if it's anywhere, it'll be in the library,' Sir Clovis replied cordially. 'Perhaps, in return for it, you'll be able to help us with a little— Oh!' he stopped when he saw Rosa.

Three serious faces turned to look at her.

Opal, Rosa thought, and her mouth went very dry.

'Is there news?' she managed to ask. 'Have they found Opal yet?'

'What? Who?' Sir Clovis looked surprised, as if he'd forgotten the day's events already. 'Oh, no – no further sightings.'

Lady Prue pulled out Rosa's chair, gesturing for her to sit down. As she did so, she noticed Dr Fielding's plain white blouse. She'd not dressed for dinner, either. Rosa was secretly pleased.

'I don't believe you've been properly introduced to Dr Fielding,' Sir Clovis said, all genial again.

'Yara,' the young woman corrected him.

'*Yara* has been working in Europe in natural history, with a special interest in extinct species.' He glanced at her. 'Is that right?'

Yara gave a tiny nod.

'Then war broke out and she was stuck in Europe, in occupied France, which, frankly, can't have been much fun for anyone, though the less said about that the better.' Sir Clovis frowned at his wine glass.

'But it is over now,' said Yara firmly. There was the tiniest hint of an accent in her voice. Her tongue wrapped itself, like a cat's tail, around certain words. 'Which is why I am going home.'

Rosa sighed. Couldn't someone, just for once, *not* be

going home? But it made her curious, and with the giant candelabra no longer blocking her view she was able to get a better look at their mysterious guest.

Despite her little round glasses, and the plait of hair wrapped across her head that made her look like a grandmother in a fairy tale, Yara was only just an adult. She had a heart-shaped face, hands that fluttered when she talked and a way of looking directly at Sir Clovis that Rosa had never managed.

A couple of times Yara caught Rosa staring at her and smiled. And, despite the bitter disappointment that this woman wasn't her mother, Rosa managed to smile back.

Dinner was a typically hearty, home-cooked affair. Luckily everyone was hungry. There was parsnip soup, followed by trout, followed by beef in a golden-crusted pie. Then Sir Clovis's favourite – apple crumble top-of-the-bowl-deep in cream. The conversation was mostly dull, grown-up stuff about the economy and bank loans; Rosa wasn't really listening. It was Yara she was interested in, Yara she wanted to hear more about.

Afterwards, as Minnie cleared the dishes, Rosa plucked up the courage to ask Yara a question.

'Where exactly is your home?' she said, because nobody had explained that part yet.

'Ah!' Yara's serious face lit up. 'Home is on the other side of the world. I'm from Brazil. Amazonia.'

'In the *jungle*? Where the jaguars live?'

'We live on the edge of the forest, yes, near the river.'

Rosa gazed at Yara in awe. 'Have you seen jaguars in

the wild? Do they really swim in the Amazon?'

'I have, and they do.'

'But you wouldn't expect one to survive in the wild around here, would you, eh?' Sir Clovis said doubtfully. 'Way too cold and damp.'

'Not to mention farmers protecting their livestock. We have cattle and sheep on our estate, and some very fine poultry,' added Lady Prue.

Yara regarded them both coolly. 'Your maid did mention that an animal escaped today.'

And Minnie would've told her exactly whose fault it was, Rosa thought, miserably.

'We had to alert the police this afternoon,' added Lady Prue.

Rosa's stomach dropped. 'Not to shoot Opal?'

'We can't risk having a wild animal on the loose,' Lady Prue replied briskly. 'And I'm sure those marksmen are a damned good shot.'

'But Mr Jarvis thinks—' Rosa stopped herself. If they'd not yet searched Westwood Moor, then she wasn't going to suggest it.

Yara, meanwhile, took off her glasses and pinched the bridge of her nose. She looked decidedly unimpressed.

'This is no way to treat an animal. To find it you must take your time. Use your eyes, and ears, and –' Yara tapped her head – 'think.'

'That might be all very well in the jungle—' Lady Prue began.

'The point is,' Sir Clovis interrupted, his good temper

beginning to fray, 'Macintyre wants his cat back, or a replacement for it, and we just don't have the money here at Westwood.'

'Perhaps it would've been wiser to take care of the animal you had,' Yara remarked.

This exact thought had been punishing Rosa all day.

'I did try!' she insisted. 'I really did try. I wrote weekly letters to Billy, the zookeeper's son, and I read all the books in the library!'

'Oh, do stop this SILLINESS!' Lady Prue snapped. 'It's no one's fault.'

'Never work with children and animals,' Sir Clovis muttered into his claret.

But, despite the clamour in her head, Rosa could still picture Opal running free. She turned to Yara.

'Would you have sent a wild animal back to the zoo?' she asked.

'I don't believe—'

'Why don't you show our guest the library?' Sir Clovis interrupted, as if fearing what Yara was about to say.

Chapter Four

Rosa was glad to escape the dining room so she could explain herself properly.

'I'd never have put Opal in danger on purpose,' she said very earnestly. 'It's just, when she heard the zoo trucks arriving, she looked so . . . *defeated*.'

Yara didn't say anything, but she seemed to be listening.

Since no fire had been lit in the library, it felt cold as they went in. The room was shabby and smelled of horsehair and leather soap, but was, without doubt, Rosa's favourite place at Westwood. It was the one room where the quiet felt comforting, where she really didn't mind being alone.

'What are you looking for?' Rosa asked.

'The works of Bernard Taverner,' replied Yara, eyes scanning the room.

'Mr B. Taverner, d'you mean?' She smiled shyly. 'That's my favourite section.'

She took Yara over to the far side of the room where the dark wood shelves reached almost to the ceiling. Though

Sir Clovis wasn't one for animals, his predecessor clearly had been, for there were hundreds of books on all sorts of creatures, many of which Rosa had never heard. The books on big cats were out of reach, but there were chairs to stand on, and Rosa dragged one over to the bookcase, then fetched another for Yara.

'Skirts are so impractical,' Yara admitted, before hitching hers up to climb onto the chair.

Teetering side by side, they studied every *B. Taverner* on the shelves. There were books on beetles, tropical butterflies, rare types of wasp that burrowed deep into tree bark and had done since prehistoric times, mosquitos, glow-in-the-dark snails, flesh-eating spiders, poisonous leeches. The books were so many they spilled over onto the shelves below: all were about the same part of the world, the Amazon jungle.

Yara, head bent, read almost every single spine. Though Rosa pretended to, she was waiting for a chance to mention Opal again.

'I've read these.' She tapped the spine of a book called *Majesty of the Jungle*, and next to it, *The Black Panther and Other Myths*. 'This one's got fascinating pictures of jaguar droppings.'

Yara pulled a face. 'Yup, that sounds like my grandfather's work. *You can't just study the pretty bits of an animal's life*, he'd always say.'

'B. Taverner is your *grandfather*?' Rosa gasped.

No one had mentioned the family connection. Yara, with her brown eyes and dark-brown hair, didn't look anything like Sir Clovis or the Taverners in the portraits.

Yara shrugged. 'I'm a sort of distant niece, I suppose. The women in our family keep their names, which makes it confusing. My grandmother belonged to the Xanti people, so I'm not entirely English, either.'

'Nor am I,' Rosa replied, pleased to find, as well as a love of jaguars, another similarity between them. She was proud to come from two countries, to have an English mother, and an Austrian-Jewish father.

Out in the hall, a door opened. Footsteps crossed the tiled floor, followed by a *thump, thump* on the stairs, as Lady Prue and Sir Clovis went up to the drawing room. They didn't have long before being summoned upstairs for coffee.

'This book you wanted . . . ?' Rosa pressed.

'Yes, sorry.' Yara focused again. 'It's a project my grandfather never finished.'

'What's it about?'

'The Giant Sloth.'

Rosa knew about the normal kind, the funny, sleepy creatures with ridiculously long toenails.

'Does it live in the Amazon?' she asked.

'Once it did, yes, over ten thousand years ago. Most naturalists believe it's extinct nowadays, but there are rumours it still exists deep in the jungle, though no one's managed to find any credible evidence.'

'Has anyone tried?' Rosa asked. Finding a jaguar on Westwood's land was proving hard enough.

'My grandfather did, and –' Yara's mouth twitched – 'a man called Professor Klaus Wiesman.'

'Together? What, as friends?'

Yara laughed drily. 'Rivals, more like! They went about it very differently – Wiesman from mostly behind a desk, my grandfather always out in the field. No wonder he never got around to writing anything up properly.'

Rosa narrowed her eyes at the shelves. She'd never seen an unfinished book in this section of the library, and she was in here most days.

'If he was still writing it, is it in a notebook?' she asked, realizing they might be looking in the wrong place.

There was a cabinet by the window that stored plans and drawings of the estate and, maybe, come to think of it, notebooks in the bottom drawer. When Rosa opened the drawer, they found ledgers, receipts, old recipe books and one small, unremarkable notebook. There wasn't a title on the cover. Yara picked it up and flicked through the yellowing pages.

'This is it.' She bit her lip, smiling. 'We've found it.'

The little book smelled of dust and something sweet, like lilies.

'Is that what the jungle smells like?' Rosa wanted to know.

Yara sniffed the pages. 'A bit, yes. And of damp and leaves and heat.'

Rosa sighed. It sounded incredible.

'So much of the jungle is unknown, which is why I'm going to try to find the Giant Sloth, and finish my grandfather's work,' Yara told her, with a firm nod of her head. 'But I want to do it carefully, to respect the forest and its people. The last thing they need is an outsider like me disturbing their way of life.'

Rosa was already lost in the adventure. She wanted to know everything: where the Giant Sloth supposedly lived, what it ate, what it looked like, how Yara would go about trying to find it in such an enormous forest.

When Lady Prue then yelled, 'COFFEE IS SERVED!' from upstairs, Yara glanced at the library door.

'Should we go up?' she asked, though didn't seem in any hurry to do so. Nor was Rosa.

'You haven't said much about your family,' she pressed. 'Will you see them as soon as you get home?'

Yara smiled. 'Ah-ha, family, this interests you, doesn't it? Yes, I'll visit my parents when I arrive. My brother and sister will be there too.'

'You've got a brother *and* a sister?' Rosa was delighted. 'What are they like? What are their names?'

'Vita and Enzo, and they'll be twelve by now. They're twins.'

'Are they nice?'

Yara's smile widened. 'Enzo's all sunshine – he's a happy, funny boy. Vita, hmmm, she's a quiet one. They were only eight when I left. It's a long time to be apart.'

Rosa chewed the end of her plait thoughtfully. Four years. It was a long time, but not as long as the seven years she'd been waiting for her family.

If she shut her eyes, she could almost imagine Yara's parents, Enzo and Vita, all living under a canopy of trees, surrounded by bright, scented flowers, birdsong, the buzz

36

of insects, their world untouched by this horrid war.

No wonder Yara couldn't wait to be back there. The evacuees had been the same, frantically stuffing clothes into suitcases when the order was given to pack. It was the noise she remembered most – twenty excited girls, all babbling at once about seeing their families again, holding their beloved pets, sleeping in their own beds, even going back to their old school.

It made her wonder what she'd do when she got home. And that was the bewildering part, because she didn't know. Sometimes, when she least expected it, she'd remember a cobbled street, a neighbour on a balcony playing the violin. She'd see the funfair in the Prater and be glad she could still recall the name of the city's park, and that the Danube, despite the waltz named after it, was grey and sluggish, not blue. Beyond these few snapshots, her memories were foggy, and growing more so. It was like trying to wipe the mirror clear after a steaming hot bath.

'ARE YOU LOST DOWN THERE? SHOULD WE SEND A SEARCH PARTY?' It was Lady Prue, again.

Yara caught Rosa's eye.

'Time to go upstairs,' she said, pocketing the notebook. 'Thank you.'

As they left the library, Yara turned to her. 'Listen, about this missing jaguar.'

'Opal.'

'Oh, dear. The animal has a name.'

Rosa frowned, not sure what Yara was getting at. 'She

belongs to my friend, Billy Macintyre. He's not a bad person, you know. He really does love her.'

'Does he?' Yara peered over her glasses. 'To understand jaguars properly, you have to see them in the forest, where they're part of nature, part of the magic. Then you'd see a zoo is no place for such an animal. Anyone who truly loves them must know that.'

Somehow, Rosa didn't think Billy *did* know. To his father, the jaguar was a money-maker, to Billy, she was a beautiful pet.

The idea rushed at her headlong.

What if she could convince Billy that Opal shouldn't be replaced, and that jaguars deserved to be free? What if this time *she* was advising him? She'd need to see a jaguar first-hand in the jungle, of course, and make a notebook of her findings just as B. Taverner had done.

It wasn't only Billy's happiness at stake here. If she couldn't convince him she'd done her best for Opal, then she'd lose him as a friend. And if she was to be stuck here at Westwood, without her family, then she definitely needed as many of those as she could muster.

It was such a crazy idea that Rosa didn't think twice about asking. As she closed the library door behind them, it came out quite naturally, quite breezily, 'I don't suppose I could come with you, to the Amazon?'

She didn't expect to be taken seriously.

Chapter Five

In bed that night, Rosa tossed and turned. Of course she couldn't go to the Amazon. It wouldn't bring Opal back, nor would it make Billy want to be friends again. And what if her mother came for her, and she wasn't here, waiting? Or a letter, telling her where her family were, and she couldn't write back straight away? Of all her silly ideas, going to the Amazon was the stupidest one yet.

Under her pillow, the little white card crackled softly. Sitting up, Rosa lit the candle by her bed and took out the card, like she often did when she couldn't sleep. On the back of it was her mother's music.

'Stars of the Forest,' Rosa murmured, tracing the title words with her finger.

The smell of Mr B. Taverner's notebook came back to her, filling her head with jaguars, ancient sloths, brown rivers and bright insects, and what being there, seeing it, *feeling it*, would be like.

Eventually, giving up on sleep, Rosa put on her dressing gown and went downstairs for a drink of water. A light showing under the kitchen door told her she wasn't the only one awake. Yara and Sir Clovis were in there, whispering. It sounded like a private conversation. Rosa hesitated, unsure whether to go in.

'The fact you're here, my dear, suggests you know the truth.' This was Sir Clovis.

'My mother told me about your arrangement, yes,' Yara replied.

Rosa stared at the door: what *arrangement*?

'I've tried writing to your father, but the letters simply get returned by that old governess, Miss Minton.'

'We call her Minty.'

'Minty . . . ah yes, of course.' He sighed, as if remembering. 'You see, I was hoping that we could come to an arrangement ourselves. You get your notebook, and, in return, you speak to your father on my behalf.'

'It won't work. I'm sorry.'

'Now look here!' Sir Clovis was starting to sound impatient. 'If we don't fix the west wing soon, it'll fall into ruin. The roof already leaks; the floors are rotted through. I could take you up there now and show you the state of it.'

Yara stayed cool. 'Where I've been in Europe there are whole *cities* in ruins. It's happening in the jungle back home too, with the farmers and the oil people destroying nature and the people's lives that depend on it. There is nothing special about your situation, I'm afraid.'

'But the funds are here to fix Westwood,' Sir Clovis persisted. 'All I have to do is sell some farmland, though because it'll mean breaking up the Westwood estate, I must have your father's permission.'

'He won't agree to it.'

'For heaven's sake, all I need is his signature on the bill of sale!' Sir Clovis was no longer whispering. 'There are developers out there willing to pay a fortune for this land.'

'I'm telling you, he won't let you sell – and certainly not to someone who wants to build on it.'

'Your father once told me if there was anything I wanted—'

'And you swore and shook hands on it. Yes, I heard. But times have changed.' Yara paused. 'Do you know what's happening to land in the Amazon, Clovis?'

'What the devil's that got to do with our leaking roof?' he cried.

A spiky silence followed.

Rosa, who'd decided this was all about money, was about to forget the glass of water and creep back to bed when the conversation changed tack.

'Minty was right about this house,' Yara said. 'It is too big and too ugly for anyone to live happily here. No wonder poor Rosa's not flourishing.'

Hearing her own name, Rosa stiffened.

'She's upset about the blasted jaguar, that's why,' Sir Clovis replied.

'It's more than that. Who is she, exactly?'

Sir Clovis's tone softened somewhat. 'Odd little creature. Came to us in '38 with the Kindertransport. Her sponsorship fell through, so we took her in.'

'She's a Jew?'

'Her father is, yes. Austrian. Her mother's English. They lived in Vienna, and thought it best to send her somewhere safe when the troubles started.'

'Has she heard from them since?'

'No.'

The beat of quiet made Rosa shiver.

'Europe is a mess – a terrible, ugly mess,' Yara said sadly. 'Nothing is back to normal. So much was destroyed by the war – train tracks, roads, telephone lines, water mains. Food's struggling to get in, people are struggling to get out or get home. Rosa must be patient.'

'Indeed, the girl *is* patient,' Sir Clovis retorted. 'She waits and waits for news but we've heard nothing.'

Yet Yara's explanation gave Rosa a fresh surge of hope. How long did it take to mend a road, a train track? A week? A month? Her family might still be here by springtime.

Sir Clovis, though, sounded more downbeat than ever.

'This *is* a sad affair. My wife and I, we're no good with children. We did hope the girl might settle, but you're right to notice: she is miserable here. What she needs is other children, animals, a bigger life. The business with the jaguar today has devastated her.'

'And you said her surname is Sweetman? Was it changed when she arrived?' Yara asked, as if thinking something through.

'Changed?'

'Made more English-sounding.'

'What? No, her mother's English anyway, so . . .'

Sir Clovis sighed. 'That word you used: *flourish*. That's the nub of it. She's like a plant in the wrong soil here at Westwood.'

Rosa frowned: was she?

All those years ago, Sir Clovis had taken her in and kept her safe from the war. And she was grateful for it. He'd fed her, and clothed her, given her a warm bed to sleep in.

But she did understand what he meant about being in the wrong soil. Maybe, when the evacuees were here, she'd been quite happy, or when she had Opal to care for and was writing letters to Billy. Then she'd felt part of a humming, breathing hive of people, almost like a family. But, now that had gone, Westwood was once more a sprawling, damp, echoing old house with too many rooms and not enough humans to fill them. In one single evening, Yara Fielding had seen that too.

'She mentioned coming with me to the Amazon,' Yara remarked.

'To Manaus?' Sir Clovis coughed in surprise. 'Good gracious, how extraordinary!'

Rosa felt stupid then. In all honesty, there was more chance of her going to the moon. So Yara's reply, when it came, completely threw her.

'Well, why not? She'd see a very different part of the world.'

'But you're doing dangerous work, aren't you, searching for this Giant Sloth?'

'She could stay with my brother and sister when I'm

working. They're her sort of age. I'm sure they'd get along.'

Sir Clovis went quiet. Rosa held her breath.

'I suppose it did help your mother after she lost her parents in that terrible accident,' he admitted, eventually.

'Actually, I was thinking more about this jaguar business,' Yara said. 'It might allow things to die down for a few weeks.'

'A visitor from Westwood,' Sir Clovis murmured, thinking aloud. 'Might be able to put in a good word with your father—'

'And a woman travelling on her own does raise eyebrows, even now. I'd appreciate her company on the journey,' Yara agreed.

Rosa gripped the door handle. They were serious about this!

'Just for a few weeks, you say?' Sir Clovis pressed.

'Yes. I'm due to return to Europe, if all goes well.'

'And you seriously think she'll want to go with you?'

Unable to contain herself any longer, Rosa burst into the kitchen. She stood startled, thrilled, blinking in the bright light.

'Yes!' she gasped. 'Oh, yes, please!'

At the table, the adults twisted round in surprise.

'Have you been listening at the door, young lady?' Sir Clovis chided.

Yara smiled, all the way up to her eyes.

'If you'd like to come with me, then that's wonderful,' she said.

Yet, just for a moment, Rosa wavered. If her mother

arrived, if she wasn't here to greet her . . . if a letter came from Austria . . .

She glanced anxiously at Yara. 'How will my family know where I am?'

'You will be coming back,' the young woman promised. 'And we do have post in the jungle . . . of sorts.'

That settled it.

In order to make the afternoon sailing from Liverpool, they'd be catching the earliest morning train from Westwood Halt.

'You'd best go and pack,' Yara advised. 'Then try to get some sleep.'

But Rosa had given up on that idea ages ago. Back in her bedroom, she ransacked her wardrobe. There were a couple of passable blouses she could take, a Fair Isle sweater, a faded corduroy skirt. Everything else, thanks to Lady Prue, was made of thick, scratchy tweed: she'd be boiled alive wearing any of it in the jungle. In the end, too excited to think straight, she knocked on Yara's bedroom door for help.

'What do people wear in the Amazon?' she fretted.

'Huh! Definitely not *those*!' Yara snorted when she saw the hideous tweed pinafores laid out on Rosa's bed.

'Good.' Rosa stuffed them back in the wardrobe. She was growing to like Yara more by the minute.

Helpfully, Yara suggested what clothes *would* be useful: the sweater 'for the boat journey', the blouses because 'mosquitos hate long sleeves', the knee socks 'for coverage'.

'From the sun?' Rosa asked.

'From ants.'

What little space was left in her suitcase was for her writing things. Once she'd made detailed notes of any jaguars she saw in the wild, she'd write to Billy. In fact, she'd write to him anyway, because she had to share her adventure with someone. Last of all, slipped carefully inside her writing pad, she packed the white card with her mother's music on the back.

When Rosa finally crawled into bed, a realization hit her. Despite losing Opal, and Billy, someone had come for her. It wasn't the person she'd expected or hoped for, but she was, at last, leaving Westwood.

Morning dawned misty and cold. In the soft, peachy light, with the Taverners on the front steps waving her off, the old house looked almost kindly.

'If my mother writes, you'll tell me?' Rosa begged Lady Prue. 'Wire me, send it on, *anything*.'

Lady Prue promised she would.

Rosa knew – everyone did – that this trip wasn't forever. As if to remind her, on the way down the lane, they passed two farm workers beating the hedgerows with sticks. It was the wrong time of year for shooting pheasants: they were obviously still searching for Opal. At Westwood Halt station, Mr Jarvis handed over her suitcase.

'Wishing you fair winds and calm seas,' he said, touching his cap. 'Be sure not to take any bananas on board ship, mind; they're awful bad luck.'

'Are they?' In all the time she'd been in England, Rosa hadn't so much as *seen* a banana: rationing had put paid to that.

She felt a sudden swirl of nerves.

What if I don't come back? she wondered. *What if something bad happens? Or something good, and I want to stay?*

She hugged Mr Jarvis doubly hard. Now she was actually leaving, it surprised her how complicated it felt.

Chapter Six

At Liverpool, their ship was already in dock. It was called the *Hilary* and had one soot-black funnel, and a hull of the same colour. Everywhere on board smelled of fresh paint and new carpets.

'Welcome, ladies! You're our first civilian passengers since the ship was refurbished,' the steward said enthusiastically, as he showed them to their cabin. 'Isn't that exciting?'

'I just hope the sea stays calm,' Rosa replied. She wasn't a good sailor. One thing she'd never forgotten about coming to England was the terrible, stormy journey across the Channel.

'Stick to drinking beef tea, poppet, and you'll be fine,' the steward assured her.

Their cabin, in tourist class, was on the upper deck. The stairs, the doors, the skirting boards and ceilings all gleamed with bright new paint.

'Did you know this ship's a war hero?' the steward said proudly, running his hand over the banister like it was the flank of a beloved horse. 'She carried our troops all over the North Atlantic during the war.'

'Gosh!' said Rosa.

'Then she's lucky not to have been torpedoed,' Yara remarked, and took the cabin key from the chatty steward. 'I thought we'd never get rid of him!' she said once he'd gone.

Yara had barely spoken to anyone – Rosa included – all day. She seemed to be very used to her own company. Rosa, who'd felt a sort of sisterly camaraderie between them back at Westwood, tried not to mind. Just being here, going to the Amazon, was more than enough.

Their cabin was barely wider than a broom cupboard. Immediately, Rosa loved it far more than her huge bedroom at Westwood. There was a bunk bed, a shoebox-sized basin, a rail behind a curtain for hanging up clothes and one small chair pulled up to a tiny desk. The toilet, reached through a sliding door, was shared with the neighbouring cabin.

In the short time it took Rosa to unpack, Yara had already started working. Books and papers, including Mr B. Taverner's scruffy notebook, lay on the small desk, and where she'd run out of room there, spread over the floor at her feet.

'I might go for a walk,' Rosa said, getting the distinct impression Yara wanted to be left alone.

More importantly, she was dying to explore the rest of the ship.

*

There wasn't much to see below deck. The dining room consisted of rows of white-clothed tables, the lounge a series of sofas and armchairs and big leafy plants. Beyond these rooms were more long, narrow corridors that led past identical cabin doors. Unsurprisingly, Rosa spent most of the rest of the day up on deck, where she witnessed the tip of Cornwall, Wolf Rock Lighthouse, then, a couple of hours later, the jagged French coastline. She'd taken the steward's advice, and stuck to drinking beef tea, and was delighted not to feel sick at all. There was so much to see, so much briny air to breathe in, that she didn't give her stomach another thought.

That evening, in the Bay of Biscay, four dolphins swam alongside the ship.

Everything looks different at sea, she wrote to Billy. *The land seems flat, and the horizon, if you look hard enough, curves. And did you know that the ocean is rarely blue? It's true! I've been staring at it all day.*

At odd times, it'd catch her, that every mile they sailed took her further from her family. It helped to think about where she was going. The books at Westwood had been full of pictures, of dark, wide rivers, trees taller than church spires, butterflies as big as blackbirds. Better still, she'd get to experience the jungle with two people her own age. She just hoped they were as friendly as Yara made them sound.

On board ship, there were only two other children among the passengers: one was a baby, who burped a lot. The other was a little boy in a sailor suit, who spoke

Portuguese to his tall, slim mother. The other passengers were mostly tourists, forever clicking away on their cameras. There was a small group of nuns, a few newly wed couples, and others, like Yara, who appeared to be going home.

'Should I learn Portuguese – the Brazilian kind?' she asked Yara that night as she changed for bed. She'd read in Mr B. Taverner's other books that it was the most common spoken language he'd come across.

Yara, still working, didn't look up.

'I want to be able to talk to Vita and Enzo.' Rosa stopped, because it was obvious Yara wasn't paying attention.

Since they'd boarded the ship, Yara had hardly ceased working. It amazed Rosa how little excitement she was showing about going home. Had it been her, she'd have been singing from the rooftops. All Yara seemed to be doing was staring at a notebook, day in, day out.

'Did you hear what I just said? About Portuguese?' Rosa asked again.

Yara finally put down her pen. 'They speak fluent English – as well as Xanti, my grandmother's language, and Brazilian Portuguese. But you'll get on fine in English.'

'Just a few phrases, then?' Rosa pressed, because she liked learning new languages. At home – proper *Vienna* home – they'd spoken three: German, a bit of Hebrew, as well as English, and Rosa dearly wished she hadn't forgotten so much of it since she'd been at Westwood.

'You could learn some silly words?' Yara raised an eyebrow. 'Enzo'll like that.'

But, reaching into her suitcase, she pulled out a battered-looking pocketbook of Brazilian-Portuguese. Briefly, Rosa wondered why Yara was carrying a phrase book in her own native language. When she opened it, there was someone else's name on the inside cover, *Leo S.*

'It belongs to a friend. I'm returning it to him,' Yara said crisply, and picked up her pen again.

On the second morning, Rosa woke to find the cabin empty. Yara had left a note: *Gone for breakfast*. It was absurdly early still – far too early for eating – and Rosa almost turned over to go back to sleep. There was a *slap* as something slid from the desk onto the floor. She opened her eyes fully.

Mr Taverner's notebook was on the carpet near the foot of her bed. It had fallen open on a page of drawings. Wriggling down the bed, Rosa reached out and picked it up. Instinctively, she sniffed the book's cover. The dusty sweet smell made her sigh. She'd never seen what was in the book properly, and the fact that Yara was spending so much time poring over it made her want to read it.

Rosa opened the notebook. The first pages were handwritten notes. The writing was so terrible she couldn't read it: squinting and turning the book sideways didn't help. The next page was more legible and written in block capitals under the heading:

CHARACTERISTICS REPORTED BY
INDEPENDENT EYEWITNESSES

Reddish brown matted fur
Rounded head
Powerful forearms
Huge claws
Over seven feet tall
Makes roaring sound
Hole/scent gland in stomach?

Note: spelling can be 'Mapinguary' or 'Mapinguari'

Tucked in the back of the book was a list of numbers that might've been coordinates or measurements – the paper was so smeared with dirt it was hard to tell. And then a map of a huge area north-west of Manaus, showing hundreds of tiny rivers like veins.

'Wow!' Rosa whispered, flicking back through the pages. 'Wow!'

It was clear, from Mr Taverner's notes, that he was convinced the Giant Sloth and this creature called the Mapinguary were the same thing, and still existed. He'd spoken to actual eyewitnesses, who'd given him descriptions:

'*We saw it late at night. It came right up to the campfire, making a terrible, screaming sound. It wasn't afraid of us or of the fire.*'

And another one:

'*The creature charged at me through the trees. I saw it coming for me – huge, like a giant ape – but terror made me sick and I fainted away.*'

On the next page were map coordinates for a group of mountain caves, located deep in the rainforest: an area where most of the Giant Sloth 'sightings' had taken place. In amongst the scrawled writing were heavily underlined words, like *clear footprints!* and *reliable witness!* Mr Taverner's excitement leapt off every page.

The idea of the Giant Sloth thrilled Rosa: it scared her too. What Yara was trying to do was going to be dangerous: the creature sounded terrifying. Yet if Yara could prove the existence of an extinct animal she'd be world famous. *Her* name would be on book covers. She'd have achieved something her own grandfather, and his rival Klaus Wiesman, hadn't. It was an incredible idea. Rosa felt proud and awed, and suddenly optimistic. If something as long-lost as the Giant Sloth could be found, then there was hope for finding her mother and Liesel.

When Yara returned from breakfast, her eyes went straight to the desk. The notebook was already back there, in its proper place. But next time Yara left the room Rosa noticed that she took it with her.

As soon as they left Lisbon, the weather deteriorated. First, the wind picked up further, then the sky turned milky, and the sea grew darker, veined with white. The ship began to sway. Things on shelves slid one way, then another. It was hard to walk anywhere in a straight line.

'I'm sorry,' Rosa sobbed, the first time she was sick.

But she soon stopped apologizing, and stayed in the bathroom, her forehead resting on the toilet seat. Then the neighbouring cabin got sick, too. Suddenly everyone wanted the bathroom all at once. There were shouts, frantic dashes, searches for buckets. Yara came back brandishing one like a trophy.

'Now get into bed and stay there,' she ordered Rosa.

Lying down with the sheets pulled tight across her chest did make her feel slightly better.

'Everyone's ill, not just you,' Yara assured her.

Later, she'd report back with tales of empty decks and deserted dining rooms, and how the few unscathed passengers would greet each other like survivors of a terrible disaster. Rosa tried to listen, but even the words 'dining room' made her feel sick.

When sleep came, it was full of feverish dreams. Instead of Opal in the stable at Westwood, it was a terrifying creature with red-brown fur that kept escaping and running into the house to find her white identity card. The first thing she did on waking was check it was safe under her pillow.

The next morning, Rosa opened her eyes to the wailing of the wind. The ship was still shuddering and lurching. She shut her eyes with a groan. When she woke again, a while later, a stranger was by her bedside. The young woman had waist-length black hair and was wearing a loose shirt and trousers.

'Hello. Feeling better?' Yara asked.

Confused, Rosa shuffled up on to her elbows. 'What—?'

Yara was no longer wearing her glasses: without them, her eyes looked bigger and brighter.

'We left Europe hours ago. This –' Yara gestured to the hair, the trousers – 'is how I dress for home.'

By lunchtime, they'd crossed the equator. Up on deck, an old sailing ritual to King Neptune was performed, but since it involved kissing a fish Rosa decided her stomach wasn't quite strong enough and stayed in bed. As the afternoon wore on, the wind dropped. The ship's movements became less troublesome, and Rosa found she could sit up for water. After that, she got better very quickly. By late afternoon, she was starving, asking for toast. And, by the evening, she was up on deck again, this time with Yara, watching a huge, tropical sun melt into the sea.

The next day was hot. The sea, a shimmering, greenish-black, stretched in every direction like silk. They saw flying fish, dolphins, and more birds than there'd been in days. On this part of the journey, Yara grew more relaxed, more sociable again.

'Can you smell it?' she asked, leaning into the sultry breeze.

Rosa caught a waft of damp leaves. Or was it soil?

A short while later, the deck grew busy. People gathered around the railings, until someone shouted: '*Terra firma!*'

On the horizon, a dark smudge became coastline. Slowly, steadily, the coast became tree-crowded, those trees, palms. A smaller pilot boat with a bright red sail came out to greet the ship.

'Is it wonderful to be home?' Rosa asked Yara eagerly. 'Oh, it must be! Tell me it is!'

'Of course!' Yara smiled, but was quickly serious again. 'Though I'm mostly here to work. Do remember that.'

Rosa hadn't forgotten. The descriptions of the Giant Sloth in Mr Taverner's notebook were very clear in her mind – clearer, almost, than those of a jaguar.

Chapter Seven

After a brief stop on the coast at Belém, the ship threaded through a busy estuary and into the tea-brown waters of the Amazon. Here, at last, they began travelling inland.

'Is this it?' Rosa asked, eyes moon-wide. 'Are we really on the *Amazon*?'

Yara smiled. 'We are. Is it not what you expected? Are you disappointed?'

'Yes! I mean, no!' Rosa insisted. And she showed Yara the pink skin on her wrist. 'I keep pinching myself – that's all.'

Less than a mile out of port, the jungle began. It was the bird calls Rosa noticed first: strange warbling sounds, whistles, a cry like a fox. The only birds visible were the vultures, who circled high above the treetops, or else sat hunched like old fishermen at the water's edge. The trees themselves were the tallest she'd ever seen, and weren't the luscious palms she'd imagined, but thin and spindly, only sprouting leaves above the forest canopy. Everything below it was a dense tangle of green.

It took a bit of getting used to, all this jungle. So did the heat. The air was thick, and when the sun came out from the clouds, Rosa could almost feel her skin steaming. In one of Lady Prue's horrid pinafores, she really would have cooked alive.

For the first couple of hours out of Belém, Yara stayed with her on deck, pointing out what Rosa otherwise might've missed.

'There's a village – look, over there,' she said as they glimpsed the eaves of a leaf-covered roof through the trees.

A few miles on, she told Rosa to watch what seemed to be a log, floating in the current. The log blinked.

'Oh!' Rosa gasped. 'An alligator?'

'They're caimans in this part of the world,' Yara told her.

A few of the other passengers had seen it too, and were pointing. The caiman, eyes and nostrils visible above the river's surface, looked faintly bored. Someone took a photograph. The little sailor boy started crying because he wanted to feed it a crust of bread through the railings.

'Are they very dangerous?' Rosa asked.

'They can kill a jaguar. And jaguars have been known to kill them.'

Try as she might, Rosa couldn't picture Opal fighting a caiman. But it was definitely something to tell Billy about in her next letter.

'Like most wild animals, they're best left alone,' remarked Yara.

The caiman seemed to agree, and with a roll of its huge, boulder-grey tail, it disappeared under the water.

The *Hilary* sailed on through the afternoon. At times, the river narrowed so much it was like travelling through a tree-covered tunnel. Then, just a mile or two later, it would widen so dramatically it'd be hard to see from one bank to the other, the water stretching away to the horizon. Then, it was like being back on the ocean again, and Rosa understood exactly why the Amazon was often known as the River Sea.

On deck, the other passengers came and went, read books, took more photographs, drank lemonade in the shade, but Rosa stayed glued to the railings. The more she saw, the more her eyes grew accustomed to the forest. There were green parrots with flamboyantly long tails, kingfishers, small white birds that looked like heron, herd after herd of little fuzzy-coated pigs.

Every now and then they'd pass a clearing where vegetables and flowers grew in the red earth. There'd be houses built on stilts for when the river flooded, and maybe, higher up the bank, smoke from a cooking fire. Sometimes, the inhabitants of these villages came out to wave or stare. A couple of times, children swam out to the boat, laughing and joking in a mix of Portuguese and another language Rosa didn't recognize. She'd smile back, trying out the few words she'd learned.

That night, the sky was starless, the dark so thick it felt as solid as a house. On deck, the lanterns drew in huge, papery moths. It was hot still, too, with just the slightest breeze coming off the water. The jungle was alive with strange screechings and rustlings. Inevitably, Rosa was soon thinking about Yara's Giant Sloth – the Mapinguary, as the people who'd seen it called it. Perhaps it was out there now, watching the boat. If she stared at the dark hard enough, she could almost see eyes glinting through the trees. It made her skin prickle. She was almost glad when Yara came on deck to fetch her for bed.

'You should've been under your mosquito net hours ago,' Yara scolded. She'd been working all evening, and looked tired. There were sweat patches on her blouse.

Inside, the cabin was unpleasantly hot. The tiny desk, once again, was awash with maps and papers. They were both lying in their bunks, with the lights off, when Yara said, out of nowhere:

'When you were sick you kept talking about your mother's music. What did you mean?'

'Oh.' Rosa sat up.

'Your pillow kept crackling too.'

Instantly, Rosa's hand went to the card. 'It's what my mother gave me, when she sent me away. I can't read music, though.'

'I can, if you'd like me to try.'

Rosa wasn't sure she was ready, but found herself saying, 'Um . . . all right.'

She switched on the cabin light. Her heart began to race as she passed Yara the music.

'"Stars of the Forest",' Yara murmured, reading the title.

Rosa nodded, hands clasped eagerly to her chest.

'Right.' Yara took a deep breath. 'Here we go.'

Her singing voice was whispery and rather flat. The song didn't seem to be particularly catchy or easy to listen to. It ended abruptly.

'Is that *it*?' Rosa asked, unable to hide her disappointment.

All this time she'd imagined a jolly, happy jig. Or a lullaby, or a song that made her heart ache for home. But this song wasn't even a *tune*. Her nose began its annoying itching. She knew she was going to cry.

'I'm sorry. I'm not much of a singer,' Yara confessed, handing back the card. 'You should ask Maia, my mother. She's got a lovely voice. You'll be meeting her soon.'

Rosa put the music back under her pillow and switched out the light, thinking her own mother would sing the song best of all.

The next morning, the landscape changed dramatically. On either side of the river, the land became flat and treeless.

'What happened to the forest?' Rosa asked Yara, who'd insisted they pack their bags early and be ready to spring ashore the second they arrived at Manaus.

Not so long ago there *had* been forest here: some of the deep undergrowth was still visible, as were the grey-stump remains of the trees. Cattle now grazed the greener stretches, which were marked out by post and rail fences like the ones at Westwood. On this part of the river there were also more houses – European ones with tiled roofs and verandas that once might've been grand family homes but whose peeling paint and dusty windows looked neglected.

'They cleared the jungle,' Yara answered. Though she was up on deck, she was still working, making notes from a map.

'Yes, I can see that—'

Yara put down her pen. 'Years ago, this whole region got stupidly rich on rubber. You'll see it in Manaus – all the big houses, the fine squares, the opera house, the shops. But now that the rest of the world's caught up people can't make money from it any more, so the jungle is being cleared for farming, oil—'

'What about the animals?' Rosa interrupted. 'And the people who lived in the forest? Where've they gone?'

'That's a very good question,' Yara admitted, but didn't have an answer.

Half an hour before Manaus, an announcement came over the ship's tannoy. They were approaching the famous Wedding of the Waters, the captain told them, where the rich brown Amazon met the dark silty waters of the river Negro. Quickly, the deck became crowded with passengers, all craning over the railings to stare at the strange spectacle in the river. Rosa found herself squashed in beside the little boy in the sailor suit, who was wailing because he couldn't see. So his mum lifted him up by his armpits and held him up over Rosa's head, saying, '*Veja! Veja!*'

The water was an incredible sight: two distinctive currents – one toffee-coloured, the other deepest brown – running alongside each other. *Like a huge slice of Sachertorte*, Rosa thought, and remembered, suddenly, a glossy chocolate cake on a stand in a shop window, and her sister, who'd been holding her hand, boasting she could eat the whole thing.

Shortly afterwards, they arrived at Manaus. The docks were teeming with all manner of boats – river cruisers, fishing boats, rowing boats, canoes. People strolled between them, selling fish, rope, newspapers, cigarettes, watermelon. After the peace of the river, it was a bustling, noisy place.

'Stay close to me,' Yara warned as the *Hilary*'s gangplank was thrown down.

Rosa nodded, suitcase in hand. They were standing near the front of the passenger queue. Yara had insisted on it. For some reason she was in a hurry to get off the boat.

After a series of clanks and shouts from the dock, a gate on board ship swung open. The passengers began to shuffle forward. Rosa took a few steps. Just in front of her was Yara. She kept her eyes firmly on the back of her head. A few more tiny steps. Behind her, someone pushed. There was a sudden surge for the gangplank. Everyone started shouting at once.

'Hey! Watch it, mister!'

'Get your hands off my suitcase!'

'There *is* a queue, you know!'

In amongst the jostling, Rosa lost sight of Yara. When she saw her again, moments later, Yara was already on the quayside. A man with slicked-back hair was trying to talk to her. He wasn't someone Rosa recognized from the *Hilary*, and Yara, arms folded, clearly didn't want to talk to him.

'Sorry! I'm coming!' Rosa cried, waving with her free hand.

As she tried to hurry, the jostling grew worse. Halfway down the gangplank, a woman in front started screaming. The gangplank tipped violently. There was a scramble of legs and arms, and an almighty splash as something hit the water. The crowd was packed too tightly together to see exactly what had gone in. Rosa hoped it was only someone's suitcase. But from the woman's frantic wailing, it obviously wasn't.

'My boy! Somebody help!' the woman cried. 'Oh, please! I beg you! He can't swim!'

In the gap under the woman's arm, Rosa caught a glimpse of the water churning next to the ship. A flash of a blue sailor suit. A dark, wet head.

The little sailor boy was drowning.

Horrified, Rosa clawed her way to the front of the crowd. She could swim: the evacuees had taught her one summer afternoon in the river at Westwood. The trick was not to think about how deep the water was beneath you.

Crawling under the gangplank rope, between bystanders' legs and shoes, she was on the brink of jumping in when another, bigger splash told her someone had beaten her to it. Arms reached down to grab the boy as he was lifted from the water. His mother snatched him to her chest.

'Bravo! Splendid job!' one of the English passengers applauded.

The other person climbing from the water, Rosa saw now, was the man who moments earlier had been talking to Yara.

'Thank you, oh, thank you!' the little boy's mother cried. 'How can I ever repay you?'

The man, spluttering, waved off her thanks. He barely looked at the boy he'd just rescued. It was Yara he was straining to get back to, and who was beckoning Rosa, very eager to make their escape.

Afterwards, in the cool, tiled chambers of the customs house, as they queued to get their papers checked, Rosa asked who the man was.

Yara's mouth tightened. '*Not* a good person.'

Which seemed an odd thing to say about a man who had just rescued a little boy from drowning.

Chapter Eight

The incident at the docks seemed to make Yara more on edge. Once their papers were stamped, she hurried Rosa through the exit and out into a busy street. The air was thick with petrol fumes, animal dung and the cries of street vendors selling little green oranges, shoelaces, cola bottles kept cool in buckets of water. After the shade of the customs house, the afternoon heat hit Rosa like a punch. Yara kept walking.

'Make sure you stay next to me this time,' she snapped.

'Sorry, I couldn't help—'

'I mean it. You don't know this city like I do.' She softened a little. 'It's just until we get to my house, okay?'

Rosa nodded. She supposed Yara was getting a bit fed up with her by now. Having a kid in tow when you were on an important expedition probably wasn't very helpful. It would only be until she met Enzo and Vita, though. She'd be spending most of her time with them, and she couldn't wait.

At the end of the street, Yara turned left. There were

no houses here at all, just blank stone walls and windows with iron grilles over the glass.

'Umm . . . Yara . . . how much further is it?' Rosa asked, panting a little.

Back on land, her legs felt decidedly rubbery. And Yara was still walking very fast, despite carrying a suitcase in the scorching heat.

'Another two hours upriver. We'll need to charter a boat to get there,' Yara replied.

Two *hours*? Another *boat*?

She'd assumed the house was just minutes away. And if it wasn't, where were they going instead?

The stern look on Yara's face put her off asking, but she felt weak, suddenly. She needed to eat. Across the street, a woman in long skirts was grilling sweetcorn ears over a fire. Rosa's mouth watered. The Westwood dinners – all the cream, the pies, the roasted meat – had never smelled this good.

She had to beg Yara to stop. But two sweetcorn ears and a delicious fried cheese dumpling later, and Rosa felt revitalized enough to keep walking. In the very next street, they came to a halt outside a tall, yellow building. Yara rapped on the door with her knuckles.

'It's a *museum*,' Rosa realized.

'Full marks,' Yara replied, because she was stating the obvious: *The Glastonberry Museum of Natural History* was painted in large letters on the door.

It was hotter than ever waiting on the doorstep. And whoever was inside seemed to be taking ages to answer the door. Rosa scratched her leg with her foot – she had been bitten last night; Yara was right about mosquito nets.

Finally, the door groaned open.

'*Sim?*' A woman's head appeared, black-eyed, black-haired, with a short, blunt fringe. Seeing Yara, her mouth fell open in astonishment. 'You came back!' she cried, and flung open the door to reveal a pair of dusty blue overalls, rather like those the zookeepers back in England had worn.

Laughing, she and Yara hugged on the pavement. Rosa hung back, shyly.

'Does your mama know you're here?' the woman asked Yara when they finally pulled apart.

'Not yet,' Yara admitted. 'I'm going to surprise her.'

Rosa felt a catch in her throat. It was going to be quite something, Yara turning up at home with no warning after four years away. It just went to show what could happen when you least expected it.

'This is Rosa.' Yara introduced her properly. 'She's my – what should I call her? – my travel companion. Rosa, this is Luella, museum curator, my oldest friend, and who I hope is about to do me a favour.'

'Oh, I am, am I?' Luella smiled, raising her eyebrows.

Yara nibbled her lip, anxious again.

'Do you mind if we come in?' she said.

They were ushered into a ground-floor room. It was dark and cool inside, and after the bright sunshine all Rosa could see initially were the outlines of tables and boxes. The air smelled of old paper and chemicals. The musty quiet reminded her of the library at Westwood. And, like the library, the museum had the feel of a place that was rarely visited.

As Rosa's eyes adjusted, she began to see the cabinets, the shelves covering every wall. Each was full of stuffed rodents, strange reptiles, birds. In every direction, glass eyes glinted at her, teeth snarled.

'Thank goodness, everything's still the same!' Yara gasped, turning slowly on the spot.

Despite Yara's obvious delight, Rosa wasn't sure what to think of so many dead animals. Then she saw the little brown dog. It was sitting on a nearby side table, looking very sweet and friendly. As Rosa went to pat it, she noticed its eyes were stuck in with glue.

'Oh!' She snatched her hand back, quick: even the dog was stuffed.

The sign underneath read: *Billy: the faithful friend of Mrs Arthur Winterbotham.* It seemed an odd choice of specimen for a natural history museum.

'Thank you for not changing anything, even the quirky bits.' Yara slipped her arm fondly through Luella's.

'I did change the name above the front door,' admitted Luella.

'By adding 'Glastonberry'? Well, I'm glad you did.'

'Ah, it'll always be his museum. I'm the guardian, that's all, now he's gone.'

Rosa must've been looking puzzled, because Yara explained: 'Professor Glastonberry was an old family friend. He died while I was away in Europe.'

'Gosh, I'm awfully sorry,' Rosa said.

Luella shushed her. 'No, no, *menina*, don't be too sad. He was a *very* old man. He died in his sleep, after lunch, in his hammock. It was very peaceful.'

Rosa's gaze fell on a set of huge, drawer-filled cabinets. They were labelled with *Rock specimens: pre-Cambrian* and *Tail plumage: Ara Ararauna* and other names she didn't understand. The one name she *did* recognize was Mr B. Taverner's, written on a drawer labelled: *Medicinal specimens.* Yara noticed what she was looking at.

'Professor Glastonberry was the only collector my grandfather trusted. Always paid a fair price, never took too much of one specimen.'

Rosa frowned. 'The animals were dead first, weren't they?'

'I should think so, yes. He was a decent man. He helped my grandfather – and my father – out of some very sticky situations.'

'And Miss Minton,' Luella reminded her.

A smile crossed Yara's face. 'Oh yes, he had a bit of a crush on old Minty, didn't he?'

Luella laughed.

Yara, though, was quickly serious again.

'This favour I need . . .' she began, then glanced past Luella to the room beyond. 'I wonder, can we have a quick look at the big chap?'

Luella led them through an archway, down some steps and into the adjoining room. It was here the 'big chap' was located. Rosa, expecting another stuffed snake, was taken aback by the sheer size of the skeleton. The creature stood on its hind legs and was so tall it almost touched the ceiling. It was balanced, somewhat precariously, on a metal stand.

'Do you know what this is?' Yara asked Rosa.

There wasn't any information with the display, so Rosa had to guess.

'A dinosaur?'

It reminded her of the pictures she'd seen in books of the *Tyrannosaurus rex*. The bones of this creature looked really ancient too, and were a grubby grey-brown colour.

'Good try. It's almost as old.'

'And as valuable,' Luella added, then looked sideways at Yara. 'Aha, *this* what your favour is about, yes?'

'It is.' Yara crouched down, opened her suitcase. When she stood up again, she was holding Bernard Taverner's old notebook. 'I'm going to finish my grandfather's work.'

Rosa, understanding, stared in amazement at the skeleton.

'Wow,' she murmured. 'So this is—'

'A *Megatherium americanum*, or Giant Sloth,' Luella finished for her. 'This specimen was found by Mr Taverner – a very, *very* good find.'

'Big, isn't it?' Yara remarked.

Big was an understatement. Rosa had no idea the Giant Sloth – or Mapinguary – was so terrifyingly huge. Did Yara really think she could track an animal this size through the jungle? And what on earth would happen if she found it?

72

Instinctively, she stepped back from the skeleton.

'It's all right,' Luella assured her. 'It won't bite you. It's only old bones.'

'*Incomplete* old bones.' Yara pointed to the creature's ribcage, where one of the bones was white, made of plaster.

Luella sighed. 'It's a good specimen, already. You don't need to find the missing rib bone.'

'I'm not talking about a rib bone. I'm looking for living proof that the sloth still exists.'

'Hmmm.' Luella frowned. 'You won't be the only one, then. A week ago a European man came in here, asking lots of questions.'

'About the sloth?' Rosa asked.

'Yes. Funny questions, really – simple, basic ones. Said a local man was working for him, and they were heading north into the jungle to follow a lead. He was a strange fish – cold, you know? The way some people are who you just can't warm to.'

Yara hesitated.

'Did you get this man's name?' she asked.

'Dr . . . it began with a W . . . He was from a top university in Europe.'

Yara's face hardened. 'Professor Wiesman, *the* Professor Wiesman, from the University of Frankfurt?'

'Yes, I'm pretty sure that's who he said he was.'

Rosa realized, with a jolt, what this meant. Mr Taverner's rival had finally stepped out from behind his university desk and was here to search for the sloth. At the same time as Yara. It was very bad timing.

'You can't give up now,' said Rosa, knowing how much finding the sloth meant to her.

'Give up?' Yara was startled. 'Ha! I've no intention of giving up. In fact, a bit of healthy competition won't do me any harm.'

'So, this favour?' Luella reminded her.

Yara passed her the old notebook using both hands, as if it was a tea tray full of cups.

'Look after this for me. I don't want to risk taking it into the jungle. It makes sense to leave it here with his collections.'

Luella took it from her. 'Is that all? No books you need from the library? No messages to send?'

'That's all. And, if anyone asks, I'm in the jungle, searching for Giant Sloths.'

Luella nodded, clutching the notebook to her chest. Something about the book caught Rosa's eye: it looked different, somehow. She'd flicked through it only a few days ago in the cabin, and it had shut easily then. Now the covers could barely close.

Something extra was inside, between the pages: a tiny corner of it, black and hard like the cover of a pocket diary, was poking out. Rosa recognized it from the customs house, earlier, when Yara had shown it to the officials. It was her passport.

Out in the street again, the afternoon sky was clouding in. Yara said they'd be lucky to make it home without a storm. They walked briskly back to the docks. Yara, head down, was silent. Rosa guessed their museum visit had given her plenty to think about, now that she knew Professor Wiesman was on the Giant Sloth's trail.

It was as they crossed the main road that Rosa noticed a man watching them. He looked familiar. His clothes, though no longer dripping with river water, were sweat-grimed, and slightly too small. The man started walking behind them. He was the same person who'd rescued the little Portuguese boy.

'Don't turn round,' Rosa whispered to Yara, 'but—'

'We're being followed. I know. I expected it.'

The man stayed about twenty paces behind.

When they reached the docks, Yara stopped suddenly and spun round to face him. The man froze, like a child caught in a party game, before tipping his hat politely. He looked, Rosa thought, rather desperate.

'You'll be wanting a boat up the river, won't you?' the man pleaded. 'I'll give you a good price, miss. The best there is.'

'I don't think so.' Yara took Rosa's arm and turned to go.

'I've a decent boat,' the man persisted. 'And who else is here to take you? You've left it a little late in the day to find anyone now.'

The man had a point. Compared to earlier, the docks were almost deserted. Apart from a couple of fishing boats and a dugout canoe, the place now seemed mostly populated by street dogs stretching themselves out to doze on the still-warm cobbles. Rosa envied them: she'd had enough of travelling for one day.

'You can trust me,' the man kept on. 'I'm a reformed character – you ask anyone, Miss Fielding.'

'*Dr* Fielding,' Yara corrected him. She looked at her watch, at the darkening sky, considering the offer. 'I suppose it *is* getting rather late.'

After a very long pause, she turned to the man again.

'All right, Mr Carter, just this once. I'm sure you know the way up the River Negro in a blindfold.'

They also knew each other, apparently.

Chapter Nine

Mr Carter was right about his boat. It was a neat, robust steam vessel, painted blue and white, with the name *Tapherini* visible on the hull. On deck, there were bench seats with cushions, and a small stove for brewing coffee. The boat seemed in far better shape than its owner. Overcome with weariness, Rosa was glad to drop her suitcase and sit down. Yara, she noticed, kept her luggage tucked between her knees. As the boat pulled away, Yara began talking to Mr Carter, confirming what Rosa had suspected.

'Are you keeping well?' she asked, having to raise her voice over the putter of the engine.

'Passable, thank you.'

'And your family? You had twin daughters, didn't you? Are they still in Europe?'

'England. Both married. It's the husbands I feel sorry for.'

Compared to earlier on the quayside, they seemed to be on almost friendly terms. It was rather odd.

'But you live in Manaus, do you?' Yara went on. 'Doing . . . what was it, again?'

Mr Carter didn't take his eyes off the river. 'Boat business, mostly.'

'This sort of thing, d'you mean, ferrying people upriver?'

'And bringing them back again, yes.'

'Interesting. You see, a friend of mine was passing through last week – a German gentleman. You might've come across him?'

Now Rosa understood what Yara was up to: she was fishing for information about the professor.

'German? No. Don't think so,' Mr Carter replied.

But all his attention suddenly switched to tending the boat's little stove. And Yara sat back in her seat, looking satisfied.

Less than an hour into the journey, darkness fell. Rosa still hadn't quite got used to how quickly the sun set here in the Amazon. It was as if a giant blackout curtain had been swished across the sky. On deck, Mr Carter lit kerosene lamps, which attracted a blizzard of insects.

'Cover your wrists and ankles,' Yara reminded Rosa.

The boat itself had a headlamp that shone out over the water, catching tree roots at the river's edge and the occasional flash of an animal's eyes. The throb of the boat's engine, the warm night air, the smell of flowers and river water all mixed together made Rosa drowsy. She fell asleep against her suitcase.

She woke with a jolt. The boat was barely moving. The engine rumbled, idling. There was a scraping sound as they slid alongside a wooden jetty, and a *slap* as ropes were thrown out for mooring.

'Are we here?' Rosa asked, rubbing her eyes.

'Yes. Make sure you've got all your things.'

They climbed off the boat on to the jetty. And from the jetty on to a narrow path, where Yara assured Mr Carter they'd be fine on their own from here.

'Are you sure you don't require a lantern?' he asked. 'I can carry your bags?'

'Mr Carter,' Yara replied, all trace of friendliness gone, 'you may not be aware that Miss Minton still lives with my family.'

'That old bat?' he gasped, then rushed to correct himself. 'I . . . I . . . mean, your mother's English governess?'

'Yes, her. It's been enough of a shock seeing you myself. I wouldn't wish it on her at her age.'

Again, Rosa wondered what the connection was with Mr Carter. Yara didn't think much of him – that was pretty clear. Rosa wasn't sure she liked him, either. It was a relief when he finally returned to the boat.

'Good riddance,' Yara muttered under her breath.

The path led away from the river, running very slightly uphill. There was no sign of a house yet. Or starlight. Or moonlight. The darkness was pitch black and bewildering. Instinctively, Rosa reached for Yara's sleeve and, finding it, held on tightly. She wasn't scared, exactly, but she did feel alert and awake. Either side of the path, leaves brushed against her. The night was noisy with insects, warbling birds, the steady drip of water. Were there jaguars here? Rosa wondered. Or other, bigger creatures that might be out there, keeping silent?

To the left of them, something crunched. A snap. The bushes crackled. There was a sound like breathing.

'What was that?' Rosa hissed.

'Probably just an animal,' replied Yara. 'Keep walking.'

'It sounds like a person.'

At that, Yara slowed. 'If Mr Carter's following us again, I swear I'll report him to the— oh!'

A shape hurled itself out of the bushes. The darkness was suddenly transformed into dazzling orange torchlight.

'Stop where you are! Don't come any further!' said a shrill voice.

Stumbling backwards, Yara lost her balance and fell. It meant Rosa now had a clear view of what was up ahead. Her heart almost stopped. Standing in the middle of the path, spear aimed directly at her forehead, was the angriest-looking girl she'd ever seen.

'GO. AWAY!' the girl ordered, coming closer.

Rosa took a shaky step back.

'We only want to reach the house,' she tried explaining, her chest tight with panic.

The girl raised her chin.

'You're with the miners, are you? Or the cattle farmers? Come on, admit it, we don't see white people out here for no reason.'

'Um . . . well . . .' Rosa flustered, desperate for Yara to stand up and explain.

'Turn round,' the girl ordered. 'And walk. We don't want you here.'

Yara, getting to her feet, burst out laughing.

'There's no denying whose daughter you are, with a temper like that!'

The girl lowered the spear. Cocked her head to one side.

'*Yara?* Is that you?'

'Yes, it's me, Vita. Shouldn't you be in bed?'

Rosa couldn't see what happened next because the angry girl dropped her torch. But there were squeals, then a sob and the sounds of two sisters hugging.

Don't think about Liesel, Rosa told herself as the tip of her nose started tingling. *Just be grateful not to have a spear pointing at your head.*

Round the very next bend in the path was Yara's family home. The house was a long, low bungalow with a thatched roof like the ones Rosa had seen from the river. At the front was a veranda, hung with lanterns and hammocks. Two of the hammocks were occupied: one by an old, thin lady who seemed to be asleep, the other by a boy who was reading a joke book.

'Hey, Vita, what's brown and sounds like a bell?' the boy called, not looking up. 'Dung! Get it?'

He turned the page, grinning.

'I've got another one—'

'Enzo?' Yara said. 'Put your book down for a second, will you?'

The boy glanced up. He had what looked like mashed potato on his chin and wide, green eyes that went even wider when he saw who it was.

'Whoa! It's the doctor!' he cried, flinging down his joke book.

He scrambled out of the hammock so fast the whole sling flipped over, tipping him onto the floor. He landed with a thump, a tangle of bare arms and legs.

'Gosh, are you okay?' Rosa asked, genuinely worried.

Vita rolled her eyes. 'He does it *all* the time. He's such a clown.'

Enzo lay on his back, laughing so much he couldn't get up.

'Glad to see you twins haven't changed,' Yara remarked, then glanced around the veranda. 'Are Mum and Dad not here?'

From the other hammock the old woman, who wasn't asleep after all, swung her legs over the edge and stood up. This, Rosa guessed, was the formidable old governess, Miss Minton. She had a bony, big-jawed face, the rest of her hidden under a shapeless dress.

'Oh, Minty!' Yara rushed over, seizing the old woman's hands in delight.

'Well, my dear, this *is* a surprise.' Minty looked a little overwhelmed.

'I'm sorry it's taken a while. Travelling across Europe is still so difficult.'

'But you made it, my dear. You're home.'

'Only for a day or two, I'm afraid.' And she told Minty and the twins about the Giant Sloth, and her mission to find one.

'Bugs alive! That's amazing!' cried Enzo.

'So you won't be staying long, then?' Vita asked, looking sullen.

'Probably not, sorry.' Yara glanced around the veranda again. 'Where *are* Mum and Dad?'

Minty grimaced. 'Ahhh . . . took off for the Xanti camp a few days ago.'

'Bit early, isn't it? The dry season hasn't started yet.' Yara turned to the twins. 'You didn't go with them?'

'Minty wouldn't let us,' Vita said, even more sullen. 'We had schoolwork to finish.'

'They didn't want the house left empty, more like,' countered Enzo. 'Too many cattle ranchers around.'

Rosa looked from one face to the other. She was having trouble keeping up.

'So?' Yara tried again. 'What happened?'

Minty freed her hands from Yara's to smooth down her dress.

'Never wear a corset in this heat – that's my advice,' she said, catching Rosa's eye.

'You're changing the subject, Minty . . .' Yara warned.

The governess gave a defeated sigh.

'You'll hear it eventually – you might as well hear it from me. There's been some trouble between your father and the cattle ranchers over land,' she said carefully. 'Your mother thought it best if they went away for a while so tempers could cool off.'

To Rosa, it sounded as if Mr Fielding – or Mr Taverner – was in the habit of losing his temper. He certainly hadn't wanted to reply to Sir Clovis's letters, not even with a polite 'no thanks'. It was Minty who'd written back.

Yara looked devastated. 'I wish Father would be more careful – he'll get himself killed one of these days.'

'He says he'll die anyway if they keep taking away the forest,' Minty said sadly, then shook her head at Yara, as if to say, *We'll talk more later*.

After supper of a delicious spicy bean stew, Yara began yawning. And then Rosa started too – huge eye-watering yawns that kept coming no matter how much she covered her mouth. The day had felt impossibly long, and though much of it had been thrilling she was tired out.

'Time for bed,' Minty declared.

Inside, the bungalow was divided into four rooms. The biggest was a living area from which three bedrooms led off, each separated by a thin timber wall. The beds themselves were hammocks draped with mosquito nets. Rosa counted only three, though Yara said she knew where the spares were kept and went off to fetch them.

It was then Rosa noticed the photograph. It was in a frame, sitting on a battered old travel trunk in the centre of the room, and was of two people with very serious faces. They both had long plaited hair and wore loose cotton shirts like the one Yara had changed into on the boat.

'Aha!' Minty said, realizing what Rosa was looking at. 'Do you see the family resemblance?'

Rosa peered closer at the picture. One of the adults definitely had Yara's heart-shaped face. There was something of Vita's fierceness there too. The other person looked so much like Enzo it was obvious they were related.

'The parents,' Rosa murmured, then she asked, 'Which is Maia?' because it was pretty hard to tell the two people apart.

'That's Finn on the left, Maia on the right. Don't be fooled by appearances,' Minty advised. 'They're two very different characters, like fire and water.'

Rosa frowned at the picture. '*Finn*, did you say?'

'Yes, the forest is in his blood. He never considered living in England when his father died, the naturalist—'

'Mr B. Taverner.'

'That's right,' Minty nodded. 'Finn stayed on. I ended up teaching both him and Maia.'

Rosa was confused. So the man in the picture, Yara's father, was also called Finn Taverner? It seemed a coincidence that he'd have the same full name as Sir Clovis, but she was too tired to ask. And by now Yara had returned with armfuls of canvas and netting, and the conversation turned to sleeping arrangements.

It was decided that all the children would share a room, despite Vita's protests. She wanted to sleep in with her elder sister. She'd barely taken her eyes off Yara all evening, sitting next to her at supper, following her from room to room. Rosa was delighted to be sharing. It reminded her of the evacuee girls, and how nice it was having someone to talk to in the dead of night.

'We don't have sheets and blankets. It's way too hot,' Enzo explained to Rosa as they watched Yara secure the hammocks.

'And too damp,' Minty added. 'All these years out here I've never got used to bedsheets. It's like sleeping under raw pastry.'

Almost as soon as she was in her hammock, Rosa began drifting off. She was aware of Minty and Yara's bedroom doors closing and, closer by, the creak of someone turning in their hammock.

'Why's she tracking a Giant Sloth, anyway?' Vita muttered. 'Why can't she stay here with us? We've not seen her for so long!'

'Because it's exciting!' Enzo replied, exasperated by his sister's disappointment. 'Because nobody really knows if they still exist! Wouldn't you want to go with her, if you could?'

'Huh! Fat chance of that.'

The twins fell silent. Vita shuffled about, trying to get comfortable.

Then, still sounding wide awake, Enzo said, 'Hey, Rosa, d'you want to hear what our father *actually* did?'

Rosa opened her eyes. 'All right.'

'He saw a farmer cutting down the forest behind our house—'

'A *cattle* farmer,' Vita added. 'They're everywhere,

grabbing the land, slashing the jungle. Vandals, that's what they are.'

Rosa turned to face the twins, which wasn't easy in a hammock. 'Why are they doing that?'

'So they can graze their big fat cows. And make money. But this lot were given even more money to clear extra land for a company searching for oil.'

'Oil? In the jungle?' This surprised Rosa.

'Yep. Worth even more than fat cows, apparently.'

'Excuse me.' Enzo cleared his throat. '*I'm* the one telling the story.'

'Sorry,' Vita muttered.

'Anyway,' Enzo carried on. 'So Dad fetched his biggest hunting spear – the one he uses for caiman – and threw it at the farmer.'

Rosa gasped. 'Did he hit him?'

'Almost.' Enzo was laughing. 'It hit the farmer's hat off his head and pinned it to a tree. You should've been there. It was priceless!'

'Not funny, Enzo,' Vita said grimly. 'It's made everything worse for us. The farmers'll get their own back. They always do. They don't care about the forest or the animals or any of us who live here.'

'Then we'll scare 'em off, won't we?' Enzo did an animal growl.

Vita snorted. 'It'll take more than that.'

Yet Rosa could still see, very clearly, Vita's spear aimed at the place between her eyebrows, and thought, impressed, *Well, you certainly scared me.*

Chapter Ten

The house was called *Renascida*, meaning 'reborn'.

'It's easier to explain in daylight,' Enzo had said, just before they'd fallen asleep.

So the next morning over a breakfast of mangoes, fresh eggs and cornbread, Rosa asked again about why the house had such an intriguing name.

'Come, I'll show you.' Enzo sprang up from his seat, all arms and legs and energy. His chair crashed to the floor behind him.

'*Enzo!*' Yara complained. 'Slow down!'

'Sorry!' He grinned sheepishly at Yara, then Rosa.

Rosa appreciated that he was trying hard to be nice – clumsy, admittedly, but nice. She was dying to ask him about jaguars too, but Minty was on her feet, draining the last of her coffee.

'Now's not the time for exploring,' she informed them. 'Lessons, dear children, start in five minutes.'

The household at Renascida had been run the same way for many years. In the rainy season, the family lived here and studied – the children at their schoolwork, the grown-ups writing about medicine and composing music. Then in June, at the start of the dry season, they'd pack up and go deep into the jungle to join the Xanti. It sounded an idyllic way to live.

'Our dad is part-Xanti,' Enzo told Rosa. 'His mother – our grandmother – was Xanti.'

'So you're quarter Xanti, yes?'

Vita nodded wistfully. 'I'd love to learn more about that side of our life, instead of books and writing and—'

'Long-dead white men,' Enzo chipped in.

Weekday lessons started at eight thirty for Vita and Enzo. Minty taught them history and geography, a smattering of maths, a great deal of poetry – particularly Keats – and the plays and sonnets of Shakespeare. Lessons were held outside on the veranda. The children were expected to be punctual and arrive with clean hands and faces. They worked at a proper table, out of proper exercise books, the pages of which wrinkled in the humidity. It was the perfect sort of classroom, as far as Rosa was concerned, with chickens pecking around their feet, parrots and butterflies swooping over their heads and the fanfare of the forest a constant background music.

'We're here until midday, so it might get a bit boring,' Enzo warned Rosa.

'It's *always* boring,' Vita replied, chin already in her hands. She'd wanted to spend the day with Yara, and clearly wasn't in the mood for lessons.

'Could Rosa join us?' Enzo suggested when Minty arrived on the veranda.

But the governess said no, not today, since they were halfway through a composition on the wives of Henry VIII. Tomorrow would be better when they started something new.

So Rosa collected her writing pad, and decided to write to Billy. It was hard to believe she'd only written a couple of days ago. She had loads more to tell him – about the Giant Sloth skeleton, Professor Wiesman, Mr Carter, meeting the twins. Though no jaguars had been spotted yet, she'd a feeling it wouldn't be long before she saw one.

Dear Billy, she began. *We've arrived! In proper jungle! Yara is going off in a day or so to search for her sloth. I'm hoping she'll teach me how to track an animal before she goes. I'm desperate to see a real jaguar . . .*

Her pen slowed. Actually, it seemed wrong to gloat about finding jaguars after losing Opal, so she crossed that part out.

At midday when lessons ended, Vita and Enzo invited Rosa on a walk.

'We'll start the tour this way,' Vita decided, indicating a track that ran from the back of the house into the forest.

'A *tour*?' Enzo pulled a face. 'Ugh, you make our home sound like a tourist attraction.'

'Rosa *is* a tourist,' Vita pointed out.

Rosa had to admit that she did feel like one. Her clothes were a bit too hot, her plaits a bit too tight. The twins with their loose hair and light cotton tops and trousers looked much more comfortable.

They set off in single file down the path, Vita leading the way, Rosa at the rear. Vita was carrying her spear again, and Enzo, a large stick. After what they'd told her about the cattle farmers, she wondered if they were expecting trouble. Or maybe there were poisonous snakes in the forest, or spiders, or monkeys that might be aggressive.

'Have either of you ever seen a jaguar?' Rosa asked. It felt easier to ask such an important question to the back of Vita's head.

'Sure,' Enzo replied.

Rosa's heart gave a little skip. 'Really? I'd *love* to see one.'

Vita stopped and turned round. 'Then be patient, and try to understand that the jungle doesn't perform on demand.'

Rosa nodded. These past years she'd got very good at waiting.

The track soon veered hard left, diving between two bushes of bright pink flowers. Just beyond was a collection of houses.

'Our neighbours,' explained Vita. 'Three families – big families of grandparents, parents, children, babies, puppies, chickens.'

'They're all our friends – even the chickens,' Enzo added.

Rosa smiled, grateful that he, at least, was being friendly.

The houses were smaller than Renascida, but with the same thatched roofs and timber-framed walls. They stood round a central firepit. The trees nearby were draped with laundry. Chickens scratched about in the dust. A man was chopping wood and singing. A group of young children crouched over a dog, tickling its stomach. When they saw Enzo and Vita, they called out:

'Hey! Tell us a joke from your book!'

'Enzo! Enzo!'

'Can we come with you?'

'Vita – *conchita!*'

They were speaking a mix of Brazilian-Portuguese and another language Rosa understood even less. Enzo beckoned them over. They came running, the dog panting at their heels.

'This is Rosa, our friend from England,' Enzo told them, then to her. 'Meet Tapi, Furo, Matteo, Josue, Beta, oh, and Julius the dog.'

Five bright-eyed faces stared at her with interest. The dog sniffed her knees.

'Hello, very nice to meet you,' Rosa said, testing out her Portuguese.

The children giggled.

'What did I say?' Rosa asked Enzo in confusion.

'You've just thanked them for the ice cream.'

Embarrassed, she tried again with slightly better results. The eldest child, Josue, nodded a greeting. The others went back to their friendly staring. The dog lay down at her feet with a grunt.

'Julius likes you,' Enzo pointed out. 'That's a good start.'

Then the man came over, an axe slung over his shoulder. His face was lined, pinched-looking. He didn't smile.

Enzo did the introductions again. The man was called Duerte. He gave a brief nod in Rosa's direction, before turning again to the twins.

'Your father did the decent thing with his spear,' he said in English. 'And we are grateful that, because of it, the cattle farmers have left us in peace these past few days. Finn has been a true friend to us and our families, but the battle isn't over – it's just beginning.'

'Do you really believe our dad *has* scared off the cattlemen?' Vita asked Enzo once they'd left the neighbours behind.

'Well, they haven't been back here since.'

'Huh! They will be!'

Vita strode on ahead, arms swinging furiously. She was clearly upset by what Duerte had said. The track was wet underfoot, and Rosa almost slipped. The walk she'd been invited on was rapidly turning into a march. She'd also noticed how, either side of the track, the forest was thinning. In amongst the living trees were ragged, splintered stumps, and on the ground sawdust where the chopping and sawing had been done. The birds were quieter here, the sunlight brighter: it felt hot on the back of Rosa's neck.

The track swung right, rose up and suddenly there were no trees at all. Rosa was stunned. It was so clear-cut, so definite, like stepping over a line. The land ahead was bare, uneven, still strewn with dead, grey leaves on what not long ago would've been the forest floor.

There *should've* been trees here. You could almost still sense them, their shadows, the shape of them. It was as if your brain was expecting to see forest. Even to Rosa, who'd never been here before, this new, bare landscape looked ugly. No trees meant no birds or monkeys cawing and shrieking. And no prey surely meant no jaguars.

'It's . . . it's . . . horrible,' she managed to say.

'See how close they're getting to Duerte's house?' Enzo said, glancing back the way they'd come.

Only a patchy band of forest stood between them and the houses. Through it, Rosa could see the thatched rooftops, the coloured splodges of laundry, the pink flowering bushes.

'A month ago, those houses were completely hidden,' Enzo told her. 'We reckon the cattle farmers are clearing twenty acres a day.'

No wonder Finn had been so furious. Rosa could almost feel it herself, rising hotly in her throat. What the farmers had done to the jungle was brutal. The whole place felt bleak, eerie, like they were standing in the aftermath of a war.

It was then Rosa sensed someone watching them. She turned, thinking Josue and his dog, Julius, had followed them. But no one was there.

Another few hundred yards and they came to a road. To Rosa's untrained eye it looked as rough as the lane down to Westwood, potholed and full of reddish-brown puddles. The road stopped abruptly a few feet from where they were standing.

'A month ago, this road wasn't here, either,' Vita remarked. 'They built it for the oil company to use.'

Rosa frowned. 'They're digging for oil here too?'

'They're going to try.'

The road was a fat orange scar cutting through the landscape as far as the eye could see. In the distance, fast-moving specks indicated vehicles were already using the route.

'And when the dry season comes they'll set fire to more land, so when grass grows back it's richer for the cattle,' Vita told her, jabbing her big toe into the earth.

'But they'll stop when they reach the houses?' said Rosa.

Enzo scratched his head. Vita rubbed her arms like she was suddenly cold.

'They *won't* stop?' Rosa cried, appalled. 'They're going to destroy those people's homes?'

Something flickered in Rosa's brain. It was of a dream she sometimes had, of standing on a staircase, the rooms above her all on fire. She knew she had to run, because something evil was in her house, trying to make her leave.

She must've looked distressed because Enzo patted her arm.

'Come on,' he said gently. 'We've plenty else to show you.'

They crossed the road and joined another path. This

time Enzo went first, beating a way through with his stick because the path was very overgrown. Without the forest canopy to block out the daylight, thorns and weeds grew thick on the ground like a strange, prickly carpet.

When they hit thick forest again, it instantly grew cooler. Under the trees, the light was green, the smell soft and earthy. Birds whistled above their heads. It felt better, walking this path. Rosa's shoulders relaxed a little, but she wasn't expecting, as the ground dipped down, to find herself suddenly back at the river again.

'This –' Enzo pointed with his stick – 'was where our mother and Minty lived with the Cut-throat Carters.'

'—eating tinned beetroot, and disgusting wobbly puddings,' Vita added.

'And those terrible twin sisters – Mum's cousins.' Enzo puffed out his cheeks. 'Honestly, some people give twins a bad name.'

The patch of ground on which they were now standing was little more than a tangle of creepers. A few white stones were still visible, marking out what might once have been a garden. Down at the river's edge, Rosa could see the rotted remains of an old jetty and, under the trees, a couple of old, sagging huts were slowly being swallowed by the jungle. There was no sign of a house.

'Why d'you call them the Cut-throat Carters?' Rosa wanted to know.

Vita rubbed her fingers. 'Money. It's why they took Mum in when her parents died: they got paid for having her.'

'Paid a *LOT*,' Enzo said knowingly. 'Minty told us.'

'They called their home Tapherini, meaning "the house of rest".' Vita snorted.

It was also, Rosa remembered, the name of Mr Carter's boat.

'So there *was* a house?' she asked.

'It burned down,' Enzo explained.

'By the cattle farmers?'

'No, an accident with a lamp and a can of cockroach killer. Renascida was built afterwards so Minty and our parents had somewhere to live. A new start – hence the name.'

'What about the Carters?'

'They went back to England,' said Enzo.

Rosa remembered hearing this on the boat, yesterday.

'Not Mr Carter, though?' she asked.

'Oh, him. He's in Manaus, somewhere. He's just been freed from prison,' Enzo said airily.

Rosa stared. '*Prison?*'

A sense came over her again that someone was watching them. She scanned the trees, the riverbank. Vita's hand, she noticed, was now resting on her spear. She too was glancing around.

'Is someone watching us?' whispered Rosa.

Vita put a finger to her lips.

Enzo, though, was struggling to keep a straight face. As they'd been talking, he'd been pushing at the long grass with his foot, and seemed to have found something. He beckoned Rosa to come closer.

'Someone's definitely got their eye on us,' he said, pointing to a particular spot on the ground.

Rosa looked down.

Stuck in the earth, peering up at her between the grasses, were three eyeballs. One eye was brown, the other two a bluish-grey with bloodshot whites. She didn't mean to, but she screamed.

Chapter Eleven

'I often wondered what happened to Mr Carter's glass-eye collection,' Minty said, a short time later on the veranda at Renascida.

The eyeballs lay on the table on a clean napkin. Now the mud had been rinsed off they didn't look particularly realistic. They were too white and round, a bit like ping pong balls. Rosa felt very stupid. And very guilty that she'd cut short their forest walk over something so silly, because as soon as she'd screamed Vita had demanded to go home.

'I don't normally scream,' Rosa insisted. She was worried they'd think her a coward – Vita, especially, who was stomping ahead. It was incredible how she managed to look angry even from behind.

'Sorry if I scared you,' said Enzo. 'I can go a bit far with the stupid jokes, sometimes.'

But Rosa had been jumpy before the eyeball incident. Seeing the ruined forest had done it, and remembering a horrid dream. There'd also been that unsettling feeling that they were being watched – all were good reasons for screaming. Still, she really wished she hadn't, and felt embarrassed.

'You do know Mr Carter's been released from prison, don't you, Minty?' Yara said as they studied Enzo's gruesome find.

'I had heard words to that effect,' Minty replied.

'We met him yesterday at the docks. He brought us back here in his boat.' She saw the disapproval on Minty's face. 'I didn't want to, but his was the only boat available.'

'And do you really think he's turned a corner since prison?'

'No,' admitted Yara. 'He's sniffing around for some reason, which was partly why I took the boat with him. Keep your enemies close and all that. Do keep an eye out for him when I'm away, won't you?'

Enzo sniggered, pointing at the table. 'Ha, keep an eye out . . . Good joke, Doctor!'

'Very amusing,' Minty said drily.

'Why would anyone collect glass eyeballs, though?' Rosa wanted to know. It wasn't as if you could *do* anything with them.

'Apparently, they can be quite valuable,' explained Minty. 'Especially if they're a pair. Mr Carter's favourites, I seem to remember, came from a famous duke, and an actress. He kept hers in a lovely blue velvet box.'

'An actress's *eyeballs*?' It sounded revolting, put like that.

'My dear, Mr Carter is *all* about money. Over the

years, he's cheated the locals out of land, withheld wages; he took in poor Maia – his own niece – purely because he was paid handsomely to do so. Every breath, every step, every look, every gesture will *always* be about money.'

Yara stepped back from the table, brushing her hands.

'Enough of Mr Carter. I'm going into Manaus this afternoon for supplies. Who's coming with me?'

'Me!' shrieked three voices all at once.

It was left to Minty to tidy away the eyeballs.

This time, they travelled in Duerte's boat. It was a long, narrow dugout that sat alarmingly low in the water. He knew all about Yara's mission to find the Giant Sloth, though no one was sure who'd told him.

'Searching for Mapinguary, eh? You won't be the first,' he said ominously.

'No,' Yara admitted. 'My grandfather tried for years.'

Duerte shook his head. 'You must understand, to see the Mapinguary is a punishment to humans who have wronged the forest. It is an evil being, too terrible to describe. The smell of it is the *stench* of death.'

'Don't you just *love* this story?' Enzo whispered to Rosa gleefully.

'I . . . don't . . . know . . .' she admitted. In Duerte's version, the beast sounded even more terrifying.

'Many of our people believe it is a true entity, young man,' Duerte remarked, overhearing. 'Your Mr Taverner was very brave – or very stupid – going after it.'

'That's why I'm using his old notes, in the hope I don't

make the same mistakes,' Yara told him.

But if that was the case, Rosa thought, then why had she left the notebook with Luella at the museum?

On arriving in Manaus, Yara headed for the main marketplace. When, without thinking, the twins and Rosa trailed after her, she stopped and told them, very firmly, that she preferred to go shopping on her own. They arranged to meet back at the boat at three.

'Can't I come with you?' Vita begged. 'Just me?'

'Not this time, sorry. Why don't you show Rosa around?' Yara suggested, then saw the look on her sister's face. 'Oh, don't make a fuss. You'll have fun.'

It was probably the worst thing Yara could've said, because, right from the outset, Vita seemed determined not to enjoy herself.

'There's nothing to see here, anyway,' she said irritably. 'The opera house is shut, the shops are half empty.'

It was a humid, sultry afternoon. The sky was black, threatening rain, and seemed to match Vita's mood.

'Is there a post office nearby?' Rosa asked, thinking she could send her latest letter to Billy.

Enzo brightened. 'Yes, and I know exactly where it is.'

He didn't, as it turned out. For a boy who could navigate the jungle so well, it soon became clear that, on busy city streets, Enzo's sense of direction failed him.

'I'm sure it's this way,' he said hopefully, leading them down a narrow side street.

Then he changed his mind, and they turned back,

crossing a main road where they had to dodge the green city trams, horses and carts, cars beeping their horns, street sellers shouting.

'Ah, I've remembered it!' Enzo cried, and dived between a gap in the buildings.

'Bugs alive, Enzo! How much further?' Vita groaned.

Enzo's shortcut brought them out on a quiet street lined with shops. There was a dressmaker, a shop selling leather luggage, a jeweller and cafes with chairs outside serving cakes whose names Rosa recognized. But Vita was right: most of the shops looked either deserted or closed.

'Where is everyone?' Rosa asked.

'It's the war, partly,' explained Enzo. 'The Europeans stopped coming to Manaus. Not many people who live here can afford these shops.'

The next street was full of brightly coloured houses – teals and yellows, oranges and pinks – which, though their paintwork was worn and flaking, was like staring at a sunset.

Then, just as Vita declared she wasn't walking another step, they found it. The sign outside said *Agencia Dos Correios*, which Enzo assured her meant post office. The building itself was grey and serious, with wrought-iron grilles over the windows, and looked so familiar that it could've been in Vienna.

'We don't *all* need to go in,' Vita insisted and sat on the front steps.

Inside, the post office was cool and echoey. Dark wooden counters ran along one wall. At the end counter was a sign Rosa recognized: *POSTA RESTANTE.*

It was probably too soon for any news from Europe. But just as it had been at Westwood every time she heard the letterbox snap, she needed to check. Once she'd posted Billy's letter, she went to the Posta Restante counter.

'Do you have any letters for a Miss Rosa Sweetman?' she asked in uncertain Brazilian-Portuguese.

To her surprise, the man nodded.

There was a moment as he passed the envelope to her when Rosa could hardly breathe. Then she saw the English stamp, the Lancaster postmark. Her heart sank: it wasn't from Vienna. The handwriting on the envelope wasn't Billy's either, which made her heart sink a little more.

The letter was from Lady Prue. No one else she knew wrote with such a wide, square nib.

'Bad news?' Enzo asked.

Rosa's nose prickled. 'It's certainly not the right news.'

She pocketed the letter, knowing all too well it might contain an update on Opal. This alone was a good reason not to read it in public, because then she really would burst into tears.

Since it was only two o'clock, and it had started to rain, Enzo suggested going to the opera house next.

'What for? It's closed,' Vita reminded them.

But Rosa, eager to take her mind off letters from home, agreed it would still be worth seeing from the outside.

As they walked, Enzo explained – because Vita clearly wasn't going to – that the city's famous opera house, the Teatro Amazonas, had been closed for over a decade. After the rubber industry crashed, most of those who'd flocked to Manaus from Portugal, Britain, America and Russia to make their fortunes went back home. The building, which had been built for their enjoyment at the end of the last century in a grand, European style, suddenly had no audience or income. This was also why the expensive shops they'd passed looked so empty.

'I've seen pictures, but that's not the same, is it?' Rosa said.

'Definitely not,' Enzo agreed.

They zigzagged back across town, stopping on a street corner to buy fried chicken, which they ate, hot and oily, straight from the pan. Thankfully, eating seemed to improve Vita's mood. By the time they reached the opera house, she'd almost cheered up.

'Well?' she asked Rosa. 'What d'you think?'

Rosa stood at the bottom of the steps, staring. She couldn't think of how to reply.

The theatre rose up like a giant, fanciful cake, making the rest of the city look plain and doll-sized in comparison. She had never seen anywhere so extravagant, not even in Vienna. The theatre's front was all pillars and arches, and tall, elaborate windows. Up on the roof was a spectacular green-and-gold dome, glistening like the scales of a fish.

'It's incredible,' Rosa finally managed.

True, the building had seen better days. Yet, despite the peeling blue paint, the boarded-up windows and weeds sprouting between the steps, it was still glorious. Rosa could easily imagine the opera in its heyday, alive with music, ticket sellers, bright lights and glittering dresses.

'Bet it's wonderful inside,' Rosa sighed, as much to herself as anyone.

Vita raised an eyebrow. 'You know the stage door is quite easy to open?'

'Is it?'

Vita nodded. Enzo rubbed his hands with excitement.

With a quick glance behind, they crept round to the back of the opera house to a paved area that smelled of drains. The stage door itself was boarded up, planks of wood nailed across it. One of these had already been partly worked loose. Using her belt buckle, Vita prised out the nail. It hit the ground with a ping. The plank swung downwards, revealing a door handle. Vita fiddled with that too until the lock crunched, and the door opened.

Vita gave a bow.

Enzo grinned. 'Brilliant!'

Rosa had to admit Vita seemed able to do anything.

'I suppose you both want me to go in first?' Vita said, flicking her hair over her shoulders.

Enzo's grin froze. 'You're really going *in*? But you don't know what might be in there.'

'I'll go first, if you like?' Rosa offered, thinking this was a chance to prove herself.

They looked at her.

'I wouldn't,' Enzo advised.

Vita smiled. 'You really want to?'

Rosa nodded, determined. 'Give me a minute's head start.'

Her heart was now pounding in her throat, but she tried very hard not to show it. If Vita realized that she wasn't really the screaming type – that she could be brave – then they might get on with being friends.

On the other side of the door was a corridor. In contrast to the outside, the whitewashed walls and stone floor were very plain. There were dressing rooms leading off the corridor, each door bearing a faded number. Everything smelled of mice and damp, reminding Rosa of the west wing at Westwood. This oddly reassuring thought kept her going.

Up ahead was a set of steps, and at the top a thick curtain that might once have been red, but now looked almost frosted with dust. Beyond it, Rosa guessed, were the stage wings. She couldn't leave without taking a look at the theatre's painted ceiling, the gold boxes where the rich people sat, the rows and rows of seats.

Halfway up the steps, she heard voices. Not Enzo or Vita, but a man, whispering angrily, and another man hissing back at him. It was coming from the stage. Rosa stopped. She recognized one of the voices. It was, she was sure of it, Mr Carter.

Chapter Twelve

She couldn't see the men at first. The light, which in the corridor had been dim, thickened to an almost-darkness in the theatre itself. Rosa sensed a huge space opening up before her, like falling into very deep water or stepping into an enormous cave. As her eyes adjusted, she recognized the shapes of seats, the dull gold of the balconies. And two hunched figures standing by the orchestra pit.

'I'm telling you, I dropped her there myself, as we agreed.' The first speaker was Mr Carter, nervous, pleading, like he'd been at the docks yesterday.

The other man was taller, panama-hatted. 'And I'm telling *you*, we paid you to watch what the doctor's up to.'

'Which I'm doing!'

'Why's she in town today, then? Go on, astound me.'

'She's looking for the Giant Sloth – that's what she's telling people,' insisted Mr Carter.

Rosa gripped the curtain. They were talking about Yara!

'She's *shopping*, you idiot,' Panama Hat growled. 'For a trip.'

'Yes, yes, she is.' Mr Carter was getting flustered.

'Tell me where she's going on this trip.'

'Upriver, tomorrow. And that's a concern because of where Wiesman—'

'DO NOT use his name!' Panama Hat pushed his face right up to Mr Carter's. 'You've never heard of him – got it? If you have to say anything, say "Odessa".'

'"Odessa" . . . yes . . . of course.'

'Good, I'm glad you understand.' Panama Hat straightened up, composing himself again. 'So what are you going to do next?'

Mr Carter hesitated. 'Follow her?'

'Ugh!' Panama Hat groaned. 'No! You find Odessa and warn them the doctor is on the trail.'

'Find Odessa? In the jungle?' Mr Carter looked concerned. 'I don't know if I'm up to that, sir. Helping him with his supplies when he arrived was one thing, but—'

Panama Hat shoved Mr Carter in the chest. He stumbled backwards, cried out. There was an almighty crash as he disappeared from view, into what Rosa guessed was the orchestra pit.

'Don't test my patience,' Panama Hat snarled.

He was walking off when, suddenly, he stopped. He'd heard something. Rosa ducked behind the curtain, wincing. She held her breath, imagining the man staring right at the spot where she crouched. The moment stretched on forever. Finally, he moved off. And Rosa, heart thundering, tiptoed back down the steps.

Outside, she was met by two very relieved-looking faces.

'You took your time,' Vita remarked as she opened the door for her.

'We thought you'd run into trouble,' admitted Enzo.

'I almost did.'

Rosa beckoned them away from the door, away from the opera house entirely. Only when they were surrounded again by the noise and bustle of the street, did she tell them what she'd overheard.

'It's Mr Carter. Yara was right not to trust him. He's being paid to follow your sister, and stop her finding the Giant Sloth.'

Vita's mouth tightened.

'Hot piranhas! I knew he was up to no good!' Enzo whistled.

'Not just him. There's also a boss man in a panama hat, who seems even nastier. They mentioned a man called Professor Wiesman – weirdly, so did Luella at the museum yesterday. Apparently he's a world expert in Giant Sloths.'

'*And?*' Vita asked.

'He's already here, in the Amazon. Sounds like he's got a head start on Yara.'

'She won't like that one bit,' Vita remarked.

'No, and they plan to keep it that way, too.'

At the docks, the boat's engine was already running. Yara was on the quayside, looking out for Rosa and the twins: when she saw them, she waved both arms above her head.

'Hurry up! We're leaving!' she cried.

They climbed on board, being careful not to sit on her shopping parcels that lay scattered across the seats. The boat rocked alarmingly. With a nod from Duerte, Yara untied the boat, and took her seat next to Vita.

'We're not late, are we?' worried Vita.

'Almost,' Yara answered. 'We need to get home as quick as we can.'

Rosa, who was sitting opposite, noticed Yara glance nervously over her shoulder. Did she know Mr Carter and Panama Hat were following her? Had she, like them, only just found out?

Something had certainly put her on edge. Enzo noticed it too, because he came right out with it.

'This is because of Mr Carter, isn't it?'

Yara blinked. '*What?*'

'Rosa overheard him just now talking about the Giant Sloth. He's being paid to stop you. He was saying –' he looked to Rosa for help – 'what was it again?'

'*Warn him the doctor's on the trail,*' she muttered, aware that Yara was now staring at her furiously. 'And Professor Wiesman is upriver—'

Yara exploded. 'STAY AWAY from Mr Carter, all of you! Do you hear me?'

Rosa flinched. She'd never heard Yara so much as raise her voice before. It was quite a shock. Vita hugged her knees. When Enzo opened his mouth to speak, Duerte revved the engine, and in a haze of petrol smoke the boat roared away from the jetty.

The journey was short, fast and very bumpy. Feeling bewildered, Rosa clung onto the side of the boat. Twice she was almost sick into the river. The afternoon rain had started falling, stinging her face and dripping into her eyes. No one dared mention Mr Carter again.

Yet the moment they were back on land, and Yara was out of earshot, Enzo pounced on the subject.

'Is Mr Carter *really* looking for the Giant Sloth?' he asked. 'It's a bit of a change from eyeballs, wouldn't you say?'

'*Ssshhhh!*' Rosa warned, though she was intrigued too.

As it was, the rain was falling harder than ever. It meant Yara, walking up ahead with Vita, couldn't hear. But Duerte, just behind them, certainly did.

'It's always this way with the Mapinguary,' he told them. 'The evil starts here, at home, spreading bad blood within a family. Nothing good will come of searching for this beast.'

Back indoors, Yara started packing for her trip straight away.

'Leave *tonight*?' Minty was startled. 'Why the rush, may I ask? This morning you were still at the planning stage of your expedition.'

'Things have changed,' Yara replied. She refused to say any more.

Rosa went to change into dry clothes. When she emerged, she saw Vita sitting, like a guard, in the doorway to Yara's bedroom. Her eyes were red from crying.

'You'll be going past the Xanti camp, won't you?' she sobbed.

Inside the room, Yara replied gently. 'I'm not sure where—'

'I saw the route on your map!' insisted Vita. 'You'll see Mum and Dad without me, so don't lie!'

Yara sighed. 'You know the risks of going to the camp, Vita. Any germs I might be carrying could be deadly to the Xanti. We have to be careful.'

'But we *are* careful,' Vita cried.

Taking Lady Prue's letter, which hadn't done well in the rain, Rosa went out onto the veranda where it was quieter. The rain had stopped, finally, but every leaf, every blade of grass was dripping wet. The paths to and from the house ran with brown water. In the surrounding forest, rain clouds floated in the tops of the trees as if caught there like cobwebs. It wasn't cold exactly – this place never was – but Rosa felt a damp chill creeping into her bones.

She looked at the wet envelope in her lap. Remembering she was trying to be braver, she slid a finger under the seal. In the short time they'd been back from town, darkness had swooped in, and she could barely see the words on the page. There was something about Mr Macintyre, Opal being missing still and the sorry state of Sir Clovis's bank balance. It was hopeless trying to read the rest: Rosa needed a lantern.

She found one hanging from the veranda roof. Since the matches were kept inside in a tin, she went back into the bungalow, where the argument between Vita and Yara was still rumbling on, by now behind Yara's closed bedroom door.

'Are they often like this?' Rosa asked Enzo, who was in his hammock, pretending to read the joke book: Rosa didn't mention that he was holding it upside down.

'Not normally, no. Vita dotes on her— oh!' He leaned closer to the wall. 'Listen to this!'

But the walls were so thin Rosa could hear everything, and Vita and Yara were shouting.

About her.

'Why can't I come with you? I'm your blood family!' This was Vita. 'You let Rosa travel with you from England, and she's a stranger!'

'That was different.'

'How?'

Heat crept up Rosa's neck.

'Trust me. It *was* different. She needed to get away from that house.'

'It's still not fair.'

'Life isn't fair, Vita!' Something slammed to the floor. 'I brought that poor girl here because she needed some friends. You could try a bit harder to be nice.'

'I *am* nice! I just want to spend time with you, not an English girl I barely know.'

'She's not entirely English.' Yara calmed slightly. 'Her father is Austrian. Jewish. Believe me, if you knew what's been happening in Europe to people like Rosa's family, you'd try a bit harder to be kind.'

'Oh, they've had their homes destroyed too, have they?' Vita cried. 'They've had their whole lives threatened, like the farmers are doing to our people?'

'Yes,' Yara said firmly. '*Now* do you understand?'

Vita fell quiet. 'Where are Rosa's family?' she asked eventually.

There was an agonizing pause. The heat reached Rosa's face. Her scalp.

'We don't know,' Yara said. 'Her English guardians have been searching for months now. No news might be good news. But it's hard to believe, even in wartime, that a woman and a teenage girl could disappear into thin air.'

'She must have a dad?'

'He left Vienna when she was a baby.'

'Is he still alive?'

'No.'

Rosa glanced at Enzo, who was staring at her with concern.

'You've gone very white,' he said. 'You'd better sit down.'

But he sounded miles away, suddenly. Rosa dropped the matches tin, turned and ran.

It wasn't a case of deciding to head for the forest. Rosa's mind was blank. All she was aware of was wet leaves, the wet path, darkness and an impossible pain in her chest. It hurt less to keep running in her sock-clad feet. Up ahead, through the trees, Rosa saw the grey-black rooflines of the neighbouring bungalows. She ran on to where the path narrowed. A low branch tore at her hair. She tripped over her own socks, now heavy with water, and fell to the ground.

Don't cry, she told herself. *Just pretend you never heard it.*

When she stood up again, she saw she was out in the open, in the weird, cleared space between the houses and the new road. She wiped her face. Took off her socks.

She'd guessed her father wasn't alive a long time ago. This wasn't a great shock. He hadn't promised to come after her. He wasn't someone she could remember. Her mother and Liesel, though, it was completely different with them.

But now they weren't coming, either. All this time she'd been waiting at Westwood, hoping for news from Vienna. Even today at the post office, she'd felt that little flare of hope.

No one had ever told her that they'd tried to find her family. No one had actually said they were missing. But when she thought of all the times Lady Prue had whisked the newspaper out of sight, or turned off the wireless when she came into the room, it was obvious. They'd tried to protect her from what was happening in Europe. It made her feel stupid and silly, like they didn't think she was brave enough to hear the truth.

The pain in her chest grew like a balloon about to

116

burst. She couldn't go back to Renascida feeling like this. Starting to walk again, Rosa soon reached the new road. Instead of cutting across it, she followed it: compared to the muddy forest it was easy walking, especially in bare feet, and in the darkness, the red, puddled soil seemed almost to glow. The light wasn't coming from the ground, she quickly realized. It was the sky, full of lightning, reflected in the rain puddles. There was no rain, no thunder, just these strange, flickering ribbons of light.

Rosa kept walking. Not knowing what had happened to her mum and Liesel was agony enough. Yet there must be someone out there who *did* know – someone who'd seen them, who'd helped them or hurt them – and that was almost unbearable.

Another light appeared, this time from between the trees that ran alongside the road. People were calling her name.

'Rosa! Where are you?'

'Rosa! Rosa!'

'Come on, Rosa, come back home and we'll talk.'

She recognized Vita's voice, Enzo's, Yara's. But she didn't want to go home, or to talk, or be found. She needed to think. Or not think. Whatever made it hurt less.

'Rosa?' A figure burst through the trees, just a few feet from her.

Panic made her step backwards off the road. She was knee-deep in bushes suddenly. Above her head, branches dripped and scratched. There wasn't a path to follow, but she kept moving, parting the leaves as if she was swimming through the forest. At first, the light trailed her.

It might've been ten minutes later, or an hour, when Rosa realized the light had stopped following. She'd no idea where she was. She listened to the forest, cricketing and croaking all around, and shivered. The jungle was awake. And so was she, with every nerve, every sense, pulled tight.

A rustling nearby in the trees grew louder. Shadows moved across the ground, and her eyes, confused, were certain she was seeing reddish-brown fur, giant claws.

Stop it, she told herself.

But the fear took hold. Heart thumping, she tried to find her way back to the road. Every tree, every bush looked the same, and she realized she was walking in circles. She was sure, now, that something was stalking her, something so big it was flattening the undergrowth as it walked.

The noise came from behind. A terrible, wailing, grating sound that made Rosa cover her ears and run. She'd never felt so cold, so scared. The beast was chasing her. It was there, at her shoulder, lumbering, grunting. And the size of it made the ground tremble under her feet.

Rosa ran deeper into the forest. She'd have kept running too, but a vine caught her ankle, and made her stumble. She put her hands out to save herself as the ground rushed up to meet her.

*

When she opened her eyes it was just getting light. The forest was full of mist and birdsong. Rosa rubbed the shoulder she'd been lying on and sat up, yawning. Any moment now last night's events would hit her all over again. She could feel it already, casting its shadow over her sleep-soft brain. Soon, she'd have to find her way back to the Renascida. Say sorry for running off, and worrying people. And she'd have to face Yara and ask what she really knew about her parents' whereabouts.

But not yet, she pleaded, because the birds were whistling, chirruping, whooping to each other. And there, up in the trees, a little grey monkey swung joyfully between the branches. Just feet from her hand, a bright red lizard skittered over the ground. Rosa took a long, slow breath: the forest felt different this morning. There was no sign of any beast. She wondered if perhaps, somehow, she'd dreamed it.

Then, a flap of wings, a warning screech. The undergrowth directly in front of her began to shake. Rosa tensed. Something was in there, moving through the bushes. She glimpsed fur. A rippling shoulder. Rosa hoped beyond hope that the sense in her gut was right, that she knew what type of animal this was.

As slowly as she could, she moved into a crouch. She waited. The undergrowth rustled and snapped. Two green-gold eyes stared out at Rosa. A dark head emerged, ears pricked, quivering.

'Hello, you,' Rosa whispered, just as she'd done so many times with Opal, when giving her a bowl of pilchards.

The leaves parted slightly. The jaguar took a half-step towards her, sniffing the air. The bowl of pilchards in this situation, Rosa supposed, was probably her, yet she didn't feel in the slightest bit scared.

If only Billy could see you, she thought, mesmerized.

The jaguar stopped about twenty feet away, still staring at her. What struck Rosa most was its size: it was longer and taller than Opal, its paws easily the size of tea plates. And the power of it – the magic – made the air prickle. No one would dare put a creature like this in a cage, or give it a nice pet name.

Though Rosa continued to keep very still, something tight began to unknot inside her. Last night's pain was easing.

'Thank you,' she whispered, 'for coming.'

The jaguar gave her a long, lazy blink, turned its shoulder and was gone.

Chapter Thirteen

The walk back to Renascida was relatively straightforward. All Rosa had to do was follow the trail she'd made last night which, in full daylight, was obviously not the work of a Mapinguary, but one very upset person, blundering through the forest.

It shocked her, rather. But she was determined to put last night behind her. Seeing the jaguar had to be a sign, didn't it, that life would be better from now on?

Dear Billy, she composed in her head as she walked. *You won't believe it, but I've just met a wild—*

She stopped.

Someone was coming through the trees. Two people. As they got nearer, she saw it was Duerte, his machete swinging. A few steps behind, looking like she'd not slept a wink, was Vita. Seeing Rosa, Duerte froze mid-swing. His free hand went to his chest.

'You are here!' he cried.

Vita darted past him to get to Rosa. A few yards from

121

reaching her, she slowed, then stopped, suddenly shy.

'You're all right, aren't you?' she asked, addressing a spot near Rosa's feet.

'I – I think so,' Rosa replied awkwardly. 'And I'm sorry I—'

'No, I'm the one who should be sorry,' Vita blurted out. 'I didn't mean to be so horrible. I'm angry at what's happening to the forest. And I'm not always very good at being friendly. Not like Enzo.'

'You're good at *everything*,' Rosa replied. 'You're clever, you know how to do things, you're brave.'

Vita's eyebrows shot up. 'Who slept in the forest last night *on her own*?'

'That was me being upset, not brave. When I'm upset, I'm not very sensible.'

'Me neither.'

They smiled at each other.

'Anyway, guess what?' Rosa was beaming now. 'I've just seen a jaguar!'

'You did, huh?'

'Absolutely. It was this close.' Rosa indicated the distance with her hands. 'It looked right at me too.'

Vita whistled, impressed.

'Perhaps we can go home now?' Duerte interrupted. He'd been waiting reasonably patiently until this point. 'It's been a long night, and I want to eat.'

'Me too,' Vita agreed, then to Rosa: 'You hungry?'

Rosa nodded. She was totally and utterly famished.

*

Back at the bungalow, after hugging Rosa and feeding her a plateful of eggs and avocado, Minty issued a stern reminder that, despite appearances, there *were* rules at Renascida.

'We act with consideration for others,' she lectured Rosa. 'And that means letting other people know if we're going into the forest. It's very easy to get lost out there.'

'Personally,' Enzo remarked, 'I think Rosa's more trouble than either of my sisters, don't you, Minty?'

'Hey!' Vita thumped him on the arm.

Rosa, who was trying very hard to be sorry, fought back a smile. In the end, Minty shooed the twins away to wake Yara, who no one could believe was still asleep. It was easier to speak sensibly once they'd gone.

'I shouldn't have run off. I'm sorry,' Rosa said, head bowed. 'I didn't mean to worry anyone.'

Checking the twins really were out of earshot, Minty sighed. 'I'll be honest, Rosa. I'd have been a little disappointed in you if you'd simply slammed your bedroom door and sulked all night. Children like you – wise, marvellous children – are inclined to act in the heat of the moment.'

Rosa looked up, blinked. 'They are?'

'Oh, yes. After raising two generations of Fieldings, I do have experience in the matter.'

Rosa blushed with pleasure. Being called wise and marvellous felt almost as wonderful as seeing the jaguar. She was still smiling when Vita and Enzo returned at speed to the veranda.

'She's not here!' Enzo cried. 'She's taken her stuff and gone.'

'Not everything,' Vita corrected him. 'She's left her big suitcase, and a mess all over the floor.'

Knowing how tidy Yara was, everyone hurried to her bedroom to see this strange occurrence for themselves. Just as Vita said, there were clothes, books, pencils strewn across the room.

'Looks like she left in a rush,' observed Enzo.

'No, that can't be right.' Minty rubbed her forehead. 'Yara agreed to stay put until we found Rosa. She was going to catch a bit of sleep then get up early to help the search.'

'I called her when we left,' Vita said. 'But when she didn't wake up, we went without her.'

'Because she'd already gone,' Enzo realized.

'Why would she agree to stay, then go anyway?' Rosa asked.

'To avoid upsetting Vita? You heard them arguing last night.'

Vita *had* desperately wanted to go with her sister – that was true. Yet Minty's stern reminder was still ringing in Rosa's ears. If Yara had meant to leave so suddenly, surely she would've told someone.

Seeing the mess on Yara's floor – the splayed books, the dishrag clothes – unsettled Rosa. She'd witnessed a scene like this before, somewhere, from a different doorway, though she couldn't think where. What she did remember was the feeling of being frightened. It was similar to the dream of fire on the staircase.

Something wasn't right here. And she was pretty sure Mr Carter was involved in some way.

'We should check outside for footprints,' Rosa decided. 'In case someone else was here too.'

Vita caught her eye, understanding straight away. 'Good idea.'

Yara's footprints were easy to spot. As small as a child's and starting just under her window, they ran all the way down the path to the river jetty.

'Why didn't she use the door?' Vita wondered.

'Didn't want to wake anyone?' suggested Enzo, giving her a pointed look.

It was, Rosa had to agree, the most likely option. There was no sign of any other, bigger, Mr Carter-sized footprints, which left Rosa both relieved and perplexed. For Enzo, it seemed to be an end to the matter.

'Lesson time,' he said to Vita, turning back to the bungalow. 'We don't want to upset Minty any more by being late.'

She glared at him. 'How can you concentrate on schoolwork when our sister is missing?'

'She's not *missing*. She's gone after the Giant Sloth.'

'Yeah, in a real hurry, without saying goodbye.'

'You're just upset she didn't take you.'

'Am not.'

Rosa, sensing a headache coming on, walked away. She couldn't shake the feeling that something *had* happened and that Vita was right.

Rounding the side of the house, she came to the shady spot where Minty kept her chickens. The mud here was still damp and in it was a set of fresh footprints. They were slightly larger than Yara's: the shoe had a flat, sandal-like sole. Frustrated, Rosa chewed the end of her plait. These footprints weren't Mr Carter's, but Minty's from when she'd collected the morning eggs.

But not all the footprints were the same size, she suddenly saw. A few were larger still, the mark in the mud suggesting stout boots or shoes. No one at Renascida wore footwear like this. Thinking she was finally onto something, Rosa followed the footprints as they looped round the chicken run like a question mark. They stopped just a few feet from the living-room window, from where you could see into the house and along the veranda. It was the perfect spot for watching Yara.

It was possible that Enzo was right, and Yara had simply left early to avoid a fuss. But someone *had* been spying here – that was obvious. After what Rosa had heard at the opera house it felt too much of a coincidence to brush it off. Professor Wiesman wanted to be the first to find the sloth, and he wasn't going to let Yara get in his way.

Anything could've happened to her.

The only way to know for sure that she was safe would be to check she'd arrived with the Xanti – and, if she hadn't, then she really *was* missing, and they'd have to raise the alarm.

She found Vita and Enzo where she'd left them, still arguing about Yara.

'Do you think Duerte would lend us his boat?' Rosa asked.

'His *boat*? Are you serious?' Enzo stared at her.

'Yes, to search for Yara. Why not?'

Vita shrugged. 'You could try, but be warned: he loves that boat like it's his favourite child.'

As predicted, Duerte's answer was a very firm no.

'Do you know how to operate a boat with a motor?' he spluttered, incredulous. 'A boat that's worth more to me than my house?'

No, they had to admit, they didn't.

The man went off, shaking his head. But he was clearly concerned about Yara's disappearance, because a short while later his son, Josue, came to find them. The sweet dog Julius was panting at his heels.

'You must use my canoe,' the boy said, pushing a pair of paddles at Vita. 'It's small but it floats.'

'Sounds promising!' Enzo grinned, though not unkindly. He stooped to give Julius a pat.

'Can we see it?' Rosa asked, which Vita repeated in Josue's language.

Together, they went down to the river jetty, where hidden underneath, between the wood slats and water, was a dugout canoe. A sharp tug on a rope, and the canoe slid out into view.

'I made it myself,' Josue explained proudly. 'For Julius and me to go on adventures.'

Just the sight of the boat set Julius off, barking and

running up and down in great excitement. But Vita and Enzo looked less convinced. There was a long pause where none of the humans spoke. With more nodding, and a gracious smile, the boy finally gave the rope to Vita.

'I'm not sure about this,' she said, fiddling nervously with the rope.

For Josue's sake, Rosa tried to be enthusiastic. But the truth was the canoe was small – *very* small, about the length of a bedroom door, and as narrow as a coal chute. For Josue, a skinny boy, about eight years old, it was fine. But she couldn't see how she and the twins would fit on board all together. Leaving someone behind wasn't an option, either.

'Could we, I don't know, travel through the forest instead?' Rosa suggested.

Enzo and Vita shared a 'don't be stupid' look.

'Okay.' Rosa understood. 'That's not a good idea.'

'The river's faster and safer,' Enzo explained. 'And we know the way to the Xanti in our sleep.'

'Would Yara have left in a boat?' she asked.

'If she's gone to the Xanti, then yes.'

But, as far as Rosa knew, Yara didn't have a boat – though Mr Carter did, which didn't exactly reassure her.

'Let's try this canoe,' she decided, because no one had come up with a better idea, and the sun was already high in the sky – time was ticking away. If Yara was in trouble, every second mattered.

Enzo agreed to climb in first.

'No laughing,' he warned, which was a bit of an ask, coming from him.

The canoe rocked only a little, then stilled. As Vita climbed in the opposite end, the boat seemed to sink.

'Oh! Too much!' Enzo cried, as water sloshed in over their legs.

But Vita didn't panic, and almost immediately, adjusting to her weight, the boat rose again and floated steadily.

'Your turn, Rosa,' Vita said, beckoning.

There was a tiny, damp space between the twins' feet. Rosa was smaller than either of them, and if the worse came to the worse, she was a decent swimmer. She braced herself.

'Ready? Hold on!' She stepped off the jetty.

It was a long, long way down.

Chapter Fourteen

Somehow, Rosa landed in the boat. One leg crumpled underneath her, the other dangled over the side, the canoe dipping perilously. Josue made frantic sculling motions, yelling, '*Observe a água!*'

Most of the water came out again. And what didn't dampened the seats of their clothes in a way that no one paid much attention to. Now they were in the canoe, they weren't getting out of it again until they reached the Xanti.

Enzo gripped his oar. 'All set?'

'All set.' Vita picked up the other oar.

Only yesterday, Vita had been begging to go to the Xanti. Now they were all going, though not for the fun of it. Both twins looked unusually nervous.

'Will you please explain to Minty where we've gone?' Rosa asked Josue. She hoped the governess would understand how urgent the trip was.

Josue nodded solemnly from the bank. At his feet, Julius the dog threw back his head and howled.

All told, it was a dignified send-off.

Though they'd little experience of operating a boat with a motor, it was obvious the twins had used a canoe like Josue's many, many times. Vita sat at the prow, paddling to her left. At the stern, Enzo paddled to the right. The little boat moved surprisingly quickly and smoothly. When water sloshed in over their feet, it was Rosa's job to scoop it out again, along with any unfortunate fish. It wasn't as hard work as paddling.

'Be our lookout,' Enzo suggested when she asked what else she could do to help. 'Any signs of Carter's boat, or that our sister's come this way—'

'I'll shout,' Rosa agreed.

Sitting up on her heels, Rosa scanned the water, the riverbank, every part of her alert. Yara had to be here somewhere. She might only be a little way ahead, round the river bend, maybe, or moored up at the next jetty.

Ten minutes passed. Then another ten. They rounded the bend, passed a couple of jetties. Ten minutes more and Rosa's hopes began to waver.

How would they know if Yara had come this way? The river gave nothing away, swirling gently around rocks and tree roots. On either bank, dense, dark green forest grew right down to the water's edge.

It would be easy to disappear in the Amazon, Rosa thought, so easy to get lost and never be found again. In remote parts of the jungle there were whole communities who'd never had contact with the outside world, and didn't want to. It wasn't so hard to believe that a long-thought-extinct creature like the Giant Sloth had managed to survive here.

'Do you want to swap, Enzo?' Rosa asked, thinking his eyesight might be better than hers. 'I could have a go at paddling.'

'You're in the wrong part of the boat,' he answered.

Thinking he meant for them to swap places, she was about to shuffle towards him when the whole boat tipped. Water swirled in over their legs.

'No!' he yelled. 'Stay exactly where you are or we'll fall in!'

In seconds, the bottom of the canoe was covered in water. Flapping about in it was a grey, round-bellied fish. Enzo drew his feet up in alarm.

'That's a piranha,' he warned. 'Mind your fingers.'

He didn't seem to be joking, but Rosa wasn't taking any chances. She grabbed the fish by its tail before dropping it, wriggling, overboard. When she sat down again, Vita was watching her.

'Now that, my friend, was brave,' she declared.

'Oh!' Rosa flushed, feeling stupid for letting the water in in the first place.

'I mean, you *have* seen a piranha bite, haven't you?'

'No.'

And, from the expression on Vita's face, she didn't think she'd want to, either.

At this point in the journey, the look of the river began to change. Though it was still wide, flanked on either side by

132

dense forest, the river channel became dotted with dozens of islets. Each one, with its own trees and little red-sand beaches, was home to nesting egrets, turtles, caiman basking in the sun. It was a beautiful part of the river, and Rosa tried to take it in so that later, when they'd found Yara and everything was all right again, she could savour what she'd seen.

The twins, meanwhile, were silent. Though it wasn't unusual for Vita, for Enzo it was definitely odd. Maybe they'd expected to find Yara by now, or at least some sign that they were on the right track.

'Are you okay?' Rosa asked him.

'Gah, I'm just hot,' he replied.

Rosa wasn't convinced.

And yet the heat was building. The sun's angle suggested it was late morning, and already rain clouds for the usual afternoon storm were bubbling up on the horizon.

'How much further is it to the Xanti?' she wanted to know.

'Another couple of hours,' Vita said vaguely.

Beyond the islets, they passed people fishing in the river, women collecting water in buckets, a fleet of small canoes like theirs, paddled by children. For a moment Rosa's spirits lifted: any one of these people might've seen Yara.

But when Vita called out to ask if they'd seen a blue-and-white river boat, or a small, dark-haired woman carrying what was probably scientific equipment, the answer was always the same: a blank stare or a vigorous no.

After another mile or two, as the river began to widen again, Vita suddenly stopped paddling, indicating that Enzo should do the same. The canoe slowed.

'It was here. I swear it was.' She manoeuvred them close to the riverbank until she was able to touch the twisted grey trunk of an enormous tree.

'It's flooded – that's why you can't see it,' Enzo replied. 'There, try behind those vines.'

The conversation went back and forth over Rosa's head for some minutes until they located what appeared to be an overgrown channel. Once they'd pushed through the outer curtain of branches, a tributary of the main river lay ahead of them. It was hard to see where this smaller river ended and the forest began, because the shorter trees and bushes were underwater.

'Everywhere along the river floods in rainy season,' Vita told her.

They passed slowly between the submerged trees. The water's surface was strewn with leaves and rotting flowers. Overhead, daylight twinkled through the forest canopy, colouring everything green and silver. It was like travelling through a strange, underwater cavern: Rosa felt slightly disorientated.

The twins, though, knew the way.

'A jacaranda tree standing between two palms,' Vita said, pointing to a clump of trees that, to Rosa, looked like all the others. 'That tells us we're getting closer to the Xanti.'

The little smile, flashed over her shoulder, was a sign

that things were finally looking up.

From now on, Rosa also had the job of lifting any stray branches or creepers that threatened to hit their heads. Before long, her arms were a mess of bloody scratches. But when she tried to wash them off in the water Enzo cried: 'Don't!'

'I'm getting the blood off.'

'Aha! That's the dangerous part,' he replied, the mischief back in his voice. 'Dad knew a man who got eaten whole by a caiman. It grabbed his arm and pulled him out of his canoe, right here, on this same stretch of water. They caught the animal the next day, sliced it open, and the man was inside.'

Rosa nursed her arms, trying to picture it. 'Not alive, though, surely?'

'No. But all in one piece without a single mark on him.'

'Nah, it wasn't a caiman that got him,' Vita argued. 'It was a seven feet tall monster that smelled of death.'

'The Mapinguary,' murmured Rosa.

'Exactly, that's what Dad told me,' Vita agreed.

From that point on, Rosa kept her hands out of the water. Sometimes there were shadows in the water around the boat. Often it was just the trees' reflections, but once Rosa glimpsed a long, scaly snout breaking the surface, and a bit later, moving through the trees, the pebbly back of a caiman at least as long as their canoe.

Then came a moment when Vita stopped paddling.

'Look!' she whispered.

Straight away, Rosa's heart leapt to her throat.

'Is it Mr Carter?' she whispered back, remembering it was also her job to keep watch. 'Which direction?'

Behind her, she heard Enzo go still. Then it was just the shriek of birds and the water dripping off the twins' raised paddles.

'*Is* it him?' Rosa hissed.

Thankfully, Vita shook her head. As she turned sideways, Rosa saw the huge smile on her face.

'Over there!' Vita pointed to where the water was rippling, about twenty feet from the canoe. 'It's a boto— Oh, I think there's two!'

Before Rosa could remember what a boto was, a sleek grey body broke the surface. Swimming beside it was a smaller, darker fish. Both were spraying water from the tops of their heads, and had long thin snouts, almost like reptiles.

'River dolphins,' explained Enzo.

Vita grinned. 'I think *boto* suits them best.'

It was true; they didn't much look like the dolphins Rosa had seen off the Portuguese coast. As they came closer, she saw the larger one wasn't actually grey at all but a wonderful blancmange pink. And, just like her and the twins, they were curious. They dived under the boat, swished their tails, rolled on their backs in the water.

It would've been so easy just to stay and watch. But after a few minutes Vita lowered her oar again; Enzo, understanding it was time to go, pushed away with his. In her head, Rosa was already thinking of what she'd tell Billy – not just about the wonder of the creatures themselves, but the quiet, respectful way the twins left them alone.

The landscape changed again as the floods began to shrink. Waxy-leaved bushes emerged, then bedraggled flowers. When the water dropped still further, the forest floor became visible, swampy and full of stagnant pools.

In some places, the retreating river wasn't much wider than a road. But not having to navigate the trees made it easier, and Vita and Enzo seemed to find a new burst of speed.

'Shortcut for the last stretch?' Vita called over her shoulder.

'Good plan,' Enzo called back.

As the river divided, they swung left along the narrower part, which was now little more than a fast-flowing stream They had to push through a bed of thick rushes, higher than the boat, higher than their heads. There were no obvious signs anyone else had been this way before them.

With a final push, they cleared the reeds. The canoe dipped as it hit deeper water again. A wave of it, colder than the river, splashed into their laps.

Enzo cried, 'Whoa!'

Vita caught her breath. And Rosa, who probably should have started scooping straight away, stared around her, stunned.

They were in a lagoon, curved like a cutlass, and full of water so clear she could see right down to the stones at the bottom. The surrounding forest thrummed with bright macaws, hummingbirds, little white birds whose name she didn't know. Flowers carpeted the ground – big, raggedy blooms that smelled almost like honey in the sunshine.

The only entrance into the lagoon seemed to be through the way they'd just come. Already the wall of rushes had closed, almost magically, behind them. Everything about the place felt secret. On the far side of the lagoon stood a small wooden shed and, running from it, a jetty. It was this the twins were paddling towards.

'Imagine living *here*!' Rosa sighed dreamily.

'Our grandad did,' Enzo replied. 'So did our dad before he met Mum and went to live with Minty. Amazing place to grow up, eh?'

'Oh, yes!' She gazed around her. It was, without question, one of the most beautiful places she'd ever seen, and about as different from Westwood as anywhere could be.

Suddenly, Vita stopped paddling.

'Uh-oh,' Enzo said under his breath.

'Shhh!' Vita whispered, tilting her head, listening. 'Someone's here.'

Thinking it might be Mr Carter, Rosa gripped the sides of the boat. Yet the sound that came drifting over the water was of a woman singing. It was so gentle it was almost lost amongst the birdsong, and she had to listen hard to hear it.

Enzo scrambled to his feet, laughing. Vita dropped

her paddle. As the left side of the canoe dipped below the surface, water began rushing in.

'Hey!' Rosa cried out. 'What the—?'

The boat tipped fully, sending them tumbling into the water in a tangle of legs. As Rosa surfaced, gasping at the cold, she saw a woman crouched at the end of the jetty. She had long, dark hair and was dangling her arms over the edge, ready to help them come ashore.

Relief flooded her.

The woman was Yara. From the eager way the twins were swimming towards her, she could hardly be anyone else.

Chapter Fifteen

The second she was out of the water Rosa realized her mistake. The woman wasn't Yara at all, but someone who looked remarkably like her.

'You're not . . . I thought . . .' Rosa's lips were so cold she couldn't get her words out.

It didn't matter. The relief on the twins' faces told her their elder sister was safe. The woman quickly explained how Yara had arrived at daybreak in a borrowed canoe.

'S-she's okay?' stuttered Rosa.

'I think so.' The woman's little frowning smile was just like Yara's. 'Though the war has made her sadder.'

It wasn't quite the reply Rosa had expected, but she understood what the woman meant.

'This,' Enzo explained, 'is our dear mama – everyone calls her Maia.'

'And you must be Rosa,' Maia said, holding out her hand.

The woman was wearing a shirt with the sleeves torn off, and a pair of enormous trousers held up with twine.

Up close, Rosa could see her dark hair was greying. She had Yara's serious, clever face, and looked, Rosa thought, rather like a pirate or a castaway or someone who'd just stepped out of the pages of an adventure story.

She shook Maia's hand, and tried not to be envious of the twins for having such a marvellous mother. Yet, once the greetings were done, Maia's expression darkened.

'You shouldn't have come,' she said.

'We had to,' Vita insisted. 'To make sure Yara was here.'

Maia softened a little. 'I know. You love your sister. But the Xanti . . . There are concerns . . . about outsiders. There was a man who passed by a couple of days ago – an unpleasant man – and it's unsettled the whole camp.'

'Was it Mr Carter?' Rosa wondered.

'Mr *Carter*? My uncle?' Maia looked surprised. 'No, it was a man called Professor Wiesman.'

The twins caught Rosa's eye. They all knew the name and what it meant.

'So he's a couple of days ahead of Yara?' Rosa asked.

'Apparently so.' Maia rubbed her forehead, then smiled again. 'But come, you're here now, and you must be tired and hungry.'

'*And* we want to see Yara,' Vita reminded her.

The camp was in a clearing. Bright, hot sunshine poured down on the palm-covered roofs of a dozen or more shelters. And it was quiet – *so* quiet even the birdsong sounded softer. The only loud noises were the *thump* and *ting* of tools. Patches of land had been worked near the shelters, and there were people there now, digging and watering. Under the shade of nearby trees, a group of women sat pounding roots to make flour.

As they entered the camp, the work paused briefly. People looked up, turned round, raised hands to shield their eyes from the sun. No one came to greet them. No one smiled. Rosa watched the twins and Maia for a sign of how best to behave. Both were looking uncomfortable, and rather crestfallen.

'They're cross with us for coming, aren't they?' Vita murmured, taking on board what her mother had said.

'*Fearful*, not cross,' Maia replied. 'You know the Xanti are a quiet, peaceful people, but that professor, he had a greedy manner, like he could take anything he wanted.'

Rosa remembered how Luella at the museum hadn't liked him much, either.

'Did he make trouble?' Enzo asked, play-boxing. 'Was there a fight? Did Dad throw another spear?'

Vita rolled her eyes. 'Enzo!'

'Or was it Orinti? He's amazing at throwing things. I saw him once hit a—' Enzo stopped when he saw Maia's face. 'What?'

'Your cousin's not been well,' she told him. 'Your father thinks the fever he has was brought here by the professor.'

Enzo dropped his fists. 'Is he badly sick?'

'He won't be up for any adventures today, that's for certain.'

Though Rosa hadn't heard the twins mention a cousin before, it was obvious Orinti meant a lot to them. Again, she felt envious of this sprawling, fascinating family. She also wondered if coming here had been such a great idea, after all. Yara hardly needed them interfering with her plans: she was more than capable of looking after herself.

'Food,' Maia announced. 'Everything will seem better once you've eaten.'

Knowing this to be true, Rosa followed as they crossed the camp to a shelter of palms where, underneath, someone lay curled up asleep on a mat. This time, Rosa was sure, it *was* Yara. As they approached, Yara sat up and rubbed her eyes.

'I might've known!' she groaned, when she saw them.

But, thankfully, she understood why they'd worried about her, and confessed Mr Carter *had* been snooping around Renascida. That was why she'd left in the middle of the night without a word to anyone, in a canoe hastily borrowed from Luella.

Wary of asking questions after Yara's outburst at the docks yesterday, Rosa stayed quiet. She was just glad nothing awful had happened. The man at the opera house in the panama hat had been pretty threatening: even Mr Carter seemed scared of him. At the start of the trip, Rosa had assumed the Giant Sloth itself was Yara's biggest danger. But it was much more complicated than that now Professor Wiesman was involved.

'You *are* still looking for the Giant Sloth, aren't you?' Enzo, who had no qualms about questions, asked. 'You're not going to let Carter put you off?'

'Enzo . . .' Maia tried to warn him. 'If your sister feels it's not right—'

'Put off?' Yara interrupted, slightly indignant. 'Of course not! My grandfather wouldn't have been intimidated by the competition, and neither am I.'

'Plus Mr Carter's made Orinti ill,' Vita said.

'We've all come here from the outside world,' Yara reminded her. 'Any one of us could pass on illness if we're not careful.'

Which meant being clean – and the twins were very clean, even at home. They took Rosa down to the nearby creek, where they washed their hands, feet, faces and the dust off their clothes. Rosa had never washed this often at Westwood.

Once they'd eaten rice and beans, everything, as Maia said it would, felt slightly better.

With the sun now directly overhead, the Xanti downed tools, retreating to the shade for an hour or so of rest. The quiet thickened, as did the heat. Hair plastered to her forehead, Rosa fell fast asleep.

When she woke, the sun had moved behind the trees. The twins' hammocks were empty. Yara was gone too. Bewildered, she tried to get out of her hammock too fast, and it tipped her out onto the ground.

'There's a knack to it,' said a voice. And there was Maia, sitting nearby on a mat. She was carving something from a piece of wood.

Rosa scrambled to her feet, dusting off her clothes. She knew she was blushing, though not because Maia made her uncomfortable. It was simply that she liked Maia – admired Maia – with a force that surprised her.

'I'm sorry. I didn't mean to sleep for so long,' said Rosa. 'Should I find the others? Are they far?'

'They've gone to find supper in the forest with their father,' Maia replied. 'They'll be back soon. Come, sit.'

She patted a place beside her on the mat. Rosa sat down, tucking her feet under her. She felt shy still, and slightly enthralled. This was probably how Vita felt when she had Yara, her big sister, all to herself.

'What do you think?' Maia held up her carving. It was a small musical instrument, similar to a penny whistle. 'Do you play anything?'

'No, I don't,' Rosa admitted. 'Though my mother was a music teacher – it says so on my travel documents, anyway.'

Maia listened, her eyes not leaving Rosa's face.

'She sent me to England with a few bars of music. I wanted to show you, but I've left it back at the bungalow.'

Saying it out loud made Rosa realize that tonight would be the first time in forever she'd slept without the card under her pillow. She felt slightly shaken.

'Music isn't something that happens on paper. It happens *here*,' Maia assured her, her fist pressed to her chest. 'You carry it inside you.'

Rosa rather liked this idea, and chewed the end of her plait thoughtfully. Though she didn't exactly understand what Maia meant about music, she knew all about feeling something so strongly it hurt beneath your ribs.

'So it doesn't matter that I can't read music?' she asked.

'Not to me,' Maia answered. Reaching out, she gently removed the lock of hair from Rosa's mouth. 'But I see how it matters to you, because it connects you to your family.'

How much did Maia know about her missing mother and sister? Rosa wondered. *What had Yara told her?*

In the trees at the edge of the clearing, a cloud of butterflies swarmed and swirled like brilliant-coloured starlings. Rosa's fingers searched her hair for another lock to chew.

'Do you see your mother ever?' Maia asked her.

Rosa frowned. '*See* her?'

'When my father died, I saw him. Not a ghost or anything spooky – it was just him, as the man he'd always been. I'd forgotten he'd gone and because I expected to see him I did.'

Rosa sighed. 'I don't remember what my father looked like.'

'What about your mother?'

'She's not dead,' insisted Rosa.

'Can you remember her, though?'

'Sometimes.' The woman she pictured was tall, slim, with cool hands. But she could never quite see her face.

'Do you think hearing your mother's music would help?'

'Yes.' Then Rosa glanced at her. 'Do you?'

146

Maia hesitated.

'Sometimes memories are difficult: you have to be ready for them,' she said carefully. 'Do you understand why you had to leave your home?'

Rosa felt the colour drain from her face.

'I have dreams,' she admitted. 'Where I'm stuck on a staircase and there's fire at the top, and sometimes I remember odd things, like books on the floor or the sound of marching boots.'

Very briefly, Maia closed her eyes.

'Did your mother give her music a name?' she asked, looking at Rosa again.

'"Stars of the Forest".'

Rosa watched Maia's mind working as she murmured the name: 'Stars of the Forest . . . Stars of the—'

Her whole face brightened.

'I know it! If you'd like me to, I'll teach it to you.'

'Oh!' Rosa swallowed in surprise. How was it possible that Maia already knew the piece?

There wasn't a chance to ask. From the direction of the forest, came the unmistakable sound of Enzo's laugh, the crack and swish as branches were pushed aside. He burst out in the open, grinning from ear to ear.

'Look what we're having for supper!' he yelled to them, holding up what looked like two enormous chickens.

Behind him was Vita, carrying two more. Then Yara, a basket on her hip. And finally, bringing up the rear, a man with an enormous beard – and a spear. Rosa guessed he was their father, the man who, she remembered now, had the same name as Sir Clovis.

'It's more than enough,' he was saying. 'We never take more from the forest than we need.'

In moments, the shelter was full of chatter and feathers and Maia pouring water for everyone. The twins' father, Finn, said a gruff 'hello'. He didn't shake Rosa's hand.

'Infection,' Vita explained. 'He's worried about Orinti's sickness.'

Rosa kept her distance. All she knew of Finn was what the twins had told her: that he had a quick temper and a very strong will. She didn't want to get off on the wrong footing, but it was obvious the twins loved their father very much. Enzo listened to everything he said without question. And Vita, she noticed, smiled much more in her father's company.

Later, Maia beckoned Rosa to a quiet spot behind a tree and gave her a pile of clothes. In it was a loose shirt like hers, trousers, flat sandals.

'Only if you want them,' she said. 'You might prefer your own clothes.'

Rosa didn't: it was a joy to peel off the sweaty skirt and blouse, better still to kick off her clumpy English shoes. In different clothes, she felt better, more comfortable, more at home.

Then Maia said: 'It's a beautiful piece that your mother wrote down for you. Let me know when you'd like to hear it.'

'Thank you,' Rosa replied. But, after all this time, she realized that she wasn't quite ready.

Chapter Sixteen

By nightfall, the mood in the camp had transformed to one of celebration. Various types of plucked bird roasted and sizzled over the central fire, and after they'd eaten there were plans for a storytelling. It was all down to the sick boy Orinti who, after hours bent double in the undergrowth, made a miraculous recovery. His illness wasn't fever after all, but the result of eating the wrong sort of berry.

All day, the Xanti's xaman, who was a tall, strong-jawed man with special knowledge of healing and spiritual matters, mashed flowers, roots and tree bark into various pastes for Orinti to swallow and then vomit up again.

'Poor thing,' said Rosa, who hated nothing in the world as much as being sick.

'But it works,' Vita insisted.

'By getting the poison out? Isn't there a nicer way of doing it?'

Finn, who was assisting the xaman, overheard her.

'*Idiota*,' he muttered.

Rosa blushed, embarrassed.

'Don't worry,' Vita whispered in her ear. '*Idiota* means he likes you. He calls my mum it all the time.'

Sure enough, the medicine worked. By the afternoon, when Orinti declared he was hungry, the camp decided to celebrate with a feast.

Much later, after everyone had eaten their fill and was sitting comfortably around the fire, Orinti began to tell a story. He was younger than the twins – about eight or nine, Rosa thought – and had Enzo's way of talking with his hands and, like Vita, was quite commanding. He put both traits to good use when, by the light of the flames, he spoke in his own Xanti language.

'Behold the Tale of the Fetid Beast!' he cried, which Vita quickly translated.

The adults laughed. There was clapping and whistling.

Enzo gave Vita a nudge. 'A story about you!'

'You're *so* funny I could die laughing,' she replied.

The youngest Xanti children growled in each other's faces, and hooked their fingers to make them claw-like. It was obviously a favourite story they'd all heard many times.

Being small, Orinti was given a block of wood on which to stand. Once he was up there, arms raised, everyone fell silent. The firelight turned his cheekbones and eye sockets into dark hollows. He became something otherworldly, like an ancient bard, Rosa thought, or a creature of magic.

Sitting right in front of him, two young children seized

each other's hands. Rosa smiled to herself, thinking of when the evacuee girls told ghost stories with the lights out, and how they insisted on holding hands. She half wondered if Vita would mind holding hers if she got scared, but decided not to.

'*Our story starts with a rebellion,*' Orinti said . . .

The Xanti language, to Rosa's untrained ear, sounded round, as smooth as pebbles. Yet with Orinti's accompanying hand gestures and dramatic facial expressions, and a few whispered explanations from Vita, she was able to follow most of the story.

'*. . . A boy and a girl are told not to stray too far into the forest because their mother is cooking a special feast to welcome home their father. The children love their papa and are excited to see him again. He's been away for a whole season, on a promise of finding gold.*

'*The children are good children and stay nearby all day, collecting flowers and fruit for the feast, and jumping off their favourite tree into the river. But, as the sun begins to set, the girl discovers a footprint . . .*'

'A footprint?' Rosa whispered to Vita. 'Is that what he just said?'

Vita nodded. 'Don't worry, it's not Mr Carter's.'

'*Despite their mother's plea not to go far, and their dear father's imminent homecoming, the children are inquisitive. This is no ordinary footprint: it is wider than a rubber tree leaf, longer than a machete. And it has just three toes.*

'*They argue about whether to investigate. It is late. Soon they'll be called home to supper. But the temptation is too strong: the children decide, foolishly, to follow the trail of footprints into the forest.'*

The smallest members of the audience gasped, eyes shining in the firelight. Personally, Rosa thought the children in the story were right to follow the footprints. For something important or spectacularly exciting, sometimes it was right to break the rules. Beside her, Vita tutted as if she was thinking the same.

But three toes.

Didn't sloths have three toes? Rosa was pretty sure they did, and started to listen more carefully. Yara, too, was sitting forward, her face in profile tense with concentration.

'The children soon realize they are trailing a monster. Instead of being wise and going home, they keep following. Like their father chasing gold, they grow excited at what finding such a monster might mean: riches, maybe, and respect from the rest of the village, who still treat them as the little children they once were, playing in the river. They become proud, our children, greedy for what might be, and this is to be their downfall.

'Soon, they are deep in the forest. It is very dark, too dark to see footprints. They are lost.'

Orinti's voice dropped a note. The pauses between words became longer, more dramatic. The hand-holding little children started to look worried. Rosa hugged her knees, aware of the darkness pressing in around them.

'It is the smell that hits them first – a terrible, sickly stench. First the boy, then the girl, begins to feel dizzy and

faint. They cannot go on. They have to sit and wait for the sickness to pass. But any wise person knows not to sit on the forest floor at night, when there are snakes and ants . . . and far, far worse. The children huddle together, terrified. The sickness gets worse. And they hear the thump of huge footsteps coming towards them.

'*The creature bursts through the undergrowth. Its smell, stronger than a rotting carcass, makes the boy pass out completely. The girl tries to stand, but her legs won't hold her. She's never seen a creature like this before. It is huge – taller than a tree, claws the size of a boat's oars. It stands on its hind legs and roars. The sound is deafening, horrifying, the cry of dying souls. And it comes not from the creature's stinking mouth but from a gaping, glistening wound in its stomach.*

'*When the children don't arrive home, the mother, father and the rest of the village go out searching. All night they follow two sets of little footprints into the forest. At first light, they find an area of flattened bushes, clumps of reddish hair caught in the trees. And a smell, like open graves, still lingering in the air.*

'*And of the two children?*

'*Nothing. Not a scrap of clothing, not a drop of blood. Just two sets of footprints that stop, suddenly, and disappear. Meanwhile, deep in the forest the evil being is peaceful again, until the next time a greedy human asks for too much.*'

A silence fell over the camp. Orinti waited, let the story settle, then bowed and stepped down from the block.

'Blimey,' Rosa muttered to Vita. 'So *that's* the story of the Mapinguary?'

'It's Orinti's version, yes – there are lots. They've all got the same sort of monster in them, with red hair and big claws, and a mouth in its stomach.'

'It's not just about monsters, Vita,' Maia, who was sitting behind them leaned forward to say. 'It's also about balance and respecting the spirits of the forest. The Mapinguary is a negative entity that takes revenge on humans who don't treat our world properly.'

'Wish they'd set one on the cattle farmers, then,' Vita replied.

'D'you think it's actually real, if all these stories describe the same thing?' Rosa asked.

'Maybe.' Vita shrugged. 'Yara thinks it's the Giant Sloth they're all describing.'

'Or,' Enzo chipped in, 'it's a just legend told to stop children wandering off into the forest.'

Rosa glanced at the twins.

'Didn't seem to stop you two,' she said, admiringly.

Though the story scared her, it hadn't stopped her, either. It'd only made her more intrigued about the search for Yara's Giant Sloth.

That night Rosa had a different sort of horrible dream: instead of a staircase she was back in the flooded forest, trying to catch something that was up ahead, just out of sight. All she knew was she had to reach it – it was life or death. But it was getting away from her, this mystery *something*. She wasn't strong enough to paddle any faster. Her arm muscles were burning. She kept calling and calling but her voice was stuck in her throat.

As the sun was rising over the trees and the twins and their parents were in various states of wakefulness, Yara declared she was leaving. Rosa was already up and dressed. A combination of Orinti's story and the exhausting dream meant she'd not slept well. Yara didn't appear to have, either. She looked tired and pale, but as determined as always. A dusty knapsack sat waiting at her feet.

'I wonder if my grandfather felt this excited before he set off?' said Yara, fingers tapping against her leg.

'Oh, I assure you, he did.' Finn was mixing something in a bowl. It smelled sweet, like lemons, but looked disgusting. He handed it to her. 'Here, for strength.'

Yara gulped it down, wiping her mouth on the back of her hand. He offered more of the same to Rosa.

'Go on. You look as if you need a drop.'

She took the bowl and swallowed the mixture. It tasted surprisingly good.

'You'll be going north-east, aiming for the high ground?' Finn asked Yara.

Yara nodded. 'That's where the caves are, according to Grandfather's notes.'

Again, Rosa wondered why she'd left the notebook behind at the museum. It seemed an odd thing to do when it contained so much information.

'I'm assuming the professor's heading that way too,'

Yara mused. 'Did he mention anything while he was here?'

Finn's jaw tightened. 'Oh, he mentioned things, all right. About the land he was going to buy, the oil he was going to drill for. It's just what this part of the world needs – another greedy European.'

'*Oil?*' Rosa didn't mean to say it out loud. But what did oil have to do with finding the Giant Sloth?

'How strange,' Yara agreed.

'No,' Finn snapped back. 'It's not. There are too many people like your professor, who come here to the jungle to take what's not theirs to take. Those blasted cattle ranchers, they're exactly the—'

'I know, Dad,' Yara interrupted, gently returning to what she needed to know. 'But did the professor say anything about where he was going?'

'I kept my distance. I still think he had a fever. There was definitely something not right about him. He kept asking if we knew about "*Odessa*". I supposed he meant the town on the Black Sea.' Finn shook his head. 'Very strange.'

Yara's face didn't change at all.

But Rosa felt her pulse quicken – she knew the word. At the opera house, Mr Carter was told to say 'Odessa' rather than mention the professor's name. It was almost a sort of a secret password, and what it all meant came to her with a jolt. The professor wasn't feverish – he was looking for someone, a person who'd also know the password, and who he was expecting to find here.

Mr Carter.

It wasn't even much of a surprise: it was more a

gnawing dread. She'd pretty much expected him to not be too far away.

Finn, though, was staring at Yara with concern. 'The drink I gave you wasn't *that* terrible, was it?'

Yara smiled weakly. 'Of course not.'

But she'd turned a very stark shade of white. Sweat beaded on her forehead as she reached for the nearest seat. 'I think I need to—'

She fainted before she could sit down.

Chapter Seventeen

There was no denying it, though Yara tried to when she came round: she was ill. Once, a few years ago, Rosa had caught the flu, but this was much more serious: so serious the xaman was called.

'Malaria?' Finn suggested, after checking Yara's tongue, her pulse, the heat of her brow.

The xaman shook his head. No, her tongue was too pink for malaria. The only sign of a bite were two small pinpricks on the back of Yara's heel. But they didn't look lumpy or itchy enough to be the work of a mosquito.

'A snakebite?' wondered Orinti. Yara had been in the forest yesterday collecting food for the feast, so it was a reasonable suggestion. Malaria or snakebite – both were frightening. Poor Vita was trying hard not to cry. She reached for Rosa's hand and held on tightly.

'Yara's not going to die, is she?' she asked.

'Of course not,' Rosa assured her. 'Your sister's as strong as—'

'An old buffalo, as stubborn as . . .' Enzo trailed off.

Even he'd given up trying to be cheerful.

Rosa was struggling to shake the feeling that this had happened on purpose – not that you could get a mosquito or a snake to bite someone deliberately. But, if Mr Carter was nearby, it all felt too much of a coincidence.

Thankfully, there were plants that could treat the fever and the stomach pains, and the xaman went off to find them. Finn was charged with making a bitter tea that cleansed the body. They needed cool water too, and Orinti, who knew where to find some, scampered off with Maia's best stoneware jug. Since the hammock was too 'swingy' and the floor 'too hard', everyone else set about making Yara a mattress out of palm fronds and moss.

'This can't be happening,' Yara sobbed, sweaty and distraught. 'I can't be ill now – I *have* to go.'

Someone tactfully pushed Yara's knapsack under a chair. It was obvious she wouldn't be leaving today for the caves. And maybe not tomorrow, either. She'd need time to recover, which, to Rosa's mind, was all the more reason to think Mr Carter was behind this.

After the application of various teas and tonics, Yara began to look a little better.

'What are you going to do about the Giant Sloth?' Vita asked.

The twins and Rosa had been sitting beside Yara, taking it in turns to fan her and give her tiny sips of water.

'Hope it hides from Professor Wiesman and waits for me until I'm fit,' Yara replied weakly.

'How far is it to the caves?' wondered Rosa.

'Two days north-east. A stretch of river, plenty of forest, and all of it going slightly uphill towards the high ground. It's where most of the sightings have been. Anyone hoping to find a Giant Sloth would start here.'

'We need a plan to slow him down,' Enzo decided. 'Like tie his shoelaces together, or steal his boots. Or we could set a trap!'

Yara's smile was more of a grimace.

'I vote we frighten him off,' was Vita's comeback. 'I could borrow Dad's spear. I'm not scared of this nasty professor.'

Rosa believed her.

But what had started as a bit of a joke from Enzo was clearly worrying Yara.

'Please don't go after him,' she begged. 'You don't know what you'd be getting involved in.'

'Like Odessa, do you mean?' Rosa hadn't meant to say it quite so directly. But it was time to share what she knew.

Yara slumped back on her pillow, closing her eyes.

'I don't know what you're talking about,' she croaked.

She wasn't a very good liar.

That afternoon, Maia suggested Rosa and the twins return to Renascida where things were quieter.

'I am missing Minty's lessons a bit,' Enzo admitted.

'*You* might be,' replied Vita. 'I vote we stay – at least until Yara's better.'

Rosa wanted to stay too. The Xanti camp was peaceful, the people – after a wary start – were welcoming. Best of all was being part of a big, vibrant family. Since she'd been here, she'd definitely thought less about her own mother and Liesel. Whether that was a good thing she didn't know, but the idea of leaving made her heart sink. It was the exact opposite, in fact, to how she'd felt about saying goodbye to Westwood.

Meanwhile, with the sun past its height, it was time to search for supper. Yara didn't look as if she'd eat anything much, but Finn insisted she needed protein.

So, with the twins bringing up the rear, Rosa followed Orinti along a track to a place where he said they'd find wild pigs and tapirs. The animals came to the spot most days to lick the salt that formed naturally in the rocks. Though she didn't say so, Rosa was squeamish at the idea of hunting a live animal, and hoped the killing part would be painless, and swiftly done by Orinti, who was the one carrying the spear. The weapon was taller than he was. Yet he was, without doubt, the leader of their little group.

'He'll be head of the Xanti one day,' Vita had told her.

The current Xanti leader, a woman with startling white hair, wasn't his mother or any relation. But she was an incredible storyteller, which was how it worked. Each generation produced a special person whose stories had the power to bind the Xanti together. Orinti was destined to be that person.

He was also, Rosa realized, very observant. Though he was walking five steps in front of her and facing ahead, he knew she was on edge – and not just about the hunt.

'There are bad spirits here,' he said, in English. 'The white men bring them, and it disturbs the forest.'

Rosa stopped. Her heart began to thump as she scanned the trees.

'Where?' she asked.

'Not today. Yesterday.'

Turning to face her, Orinti mimed the combing back of his hair. The twins had caught up by now, and Enzo, recognizing the gesture, named Mr Carter straight away. A confirmed sighting, then. He'd been seen here, when Yara was in the forest.

'Have you looked at the mark on Yara's leg? Properly, I mean,' Rosa said, sharing what had been worrying her.

'The bite?' Vita asked.

'What if it isn't a bite?' she answered. 'What if it's something Mr Carter's done to her to stop her finding the sloth?'

Vita looked alarmed.

'Hot piranhas!' gasped Enzo. 'Like a poison dart? Has anyone told Dad?'

The words had barely left his mouth when Vita pushed past him, and ran back towards the camp. Rosa went after her, the others close at her heels.

Already, it looked as if they might be too late. In the short time they'd been gone, Yara had taken a turn for the worse. They found her unconscious, lying so still Rosa wasn't sure her chest was moving in and out. It was hard to believe she was still alive. The shock of it made her dizzy.

Crouched beside the bed, Maia was smoothing the hair off Yara's forehead. Helpless, Finn and the xaman looked on.

'I do not understand,' the xaman muttered. 'I tried snakebite remedies, mosquito, frog, ant – everything.'

'But it might not be a bite,' Vita insisted, echoing what Rosa had just told her, then to her father. 'Dad, have another look – go on!'

Finn wasn't convinced. But with Vita and Rosa's help, he managed to turn Yara's foot so they could see it properly. The skin was burning hot to the touch. Two bright red circles surrounded the original marks.

Rosa gasped. She knew what insect bites looked like: there'd been horseflies aplenty back in England. And, to start with, Yara's wound *had* looked like a bite, but it didn't any more.

They waited, impatient, as the xaman inspected the wound for himself.

'*Could* it be a dart?' asked Vita. She was holding Rosa's hand again, much to Rosa's relief.

'Curare,' the man said under his breath. 'Like the monkey hunters use.'

Finn looked visibly shocked. 'Who in their right mind would want to poison Yara?'

There was an awkward silence. Finn stared directly at Vita.

'What do you know about this?' he demanded.

Vita reddened. When Finn saw the sideways glance

163

she gave Rosa, he turned to her instead.

'Rosa.' His voice was low and angry. 'If you've any idea what business our daughter is caught up in, then you'd better say so, right now.'

'Steady, Finn,' Maia warned. 'This isn't Rosa's fault.'

But Rosa straightened her shoulders.

'Professor Wiesman wants to find the Giant Sloth *very* badly. Mr Carter is working for him, and won't stop at anything,' she said, and told them the rest of what she'd overheard.

'Carter, I *knew* it!' Finn was furious.

Despite the fact Mr Carter wasn't his uncle, he took the news far worse than Maia, who retreated quietly behind her hair.

'A hunting dart? On my daughter? Wait till I get my hands on that *monster*!' Finn thundered.

Rosa winced. *This* was the Finn she'd heard about, the man with the red-hot temper. But she understood his reaction. Something – someone – he loved had been threatened.

'Yams and tawari bark – we will try those next,' the xaman decided, and went quickly into the forest.

Finn followed.

'Go with them, Vita,' Maia said gently. 'Make sure your father is all right.'

Reluctantly, Vita let go of Rosa, and with a final, tearful glance at Yara she went after her father. Rosa sat down next to the bed. She was struggling to believe what Mr Carter had done.

What if Yara *did* die?

No, she couldn't think about that, not after she'd promised Vita that her sister would recover. But Yara looked so ill, sweat rolling off her forehead, soaking the pillow. Rosa couldn't bear it. She covered her face with her hands.

At first, the singing was so quiet she assumed it was a bird in the forest. As it grew louder, she looked up and saw it was Maia. The song was lovely, wordless, its tune light and swirling. If the music was a colour, it would be yellow, she decided. If it was a dance, it would be something fast and giddy, like a waltz. As for food, it would be whipped vanilla cream, or a lemon sherbet that fizzed on your tongue.

She didn't want the song to stop, but eventually it did.

'Well?' Maia asked. 'Did you like it?'

'Yes.'

'How did it make you feel?'

'Like I wanted to follow my feet, or look at the sky.'

Maia's face lit up. 'That's exactly it! I first heard that song in dancing classes when I was a girl. My cousins thought I was just showing off, but I wasn't – it was the music, telling me to move how I wanted, to let my heart and my feet decide.'

'What's the song called?'

'"Stars of the Forest". It's an old, old classic.'

Rosa frowned, thinking. 'Why would my mother send me away with this particular song?'

'Maybe she wanted you to know of it, or that hearing

it might bring back some memories?'

It was possible – probable, even.

As Yara lay between them in a deep, desperate sleep, Maia suggested teaching Rosa the song.

'A little music might help us all,' she declared.

They began slowly, softly, a few bars at a time. To Rosa's surprise, she picked up the tune quite quickly, and before long it was sparkling in her head. But that was all it did – sparkle and shine. She'd been hoping for the music to trigger a memory of her mother dancing or Liesel playing the song on the piano – did they *have* a piano? Even that, she wasn't sure about.

'I still don't understand,' Rosa said eventually. 'What's this song meant to mean?'

Maia didn't answer.

At first, Rosa thought she hadn't heard the question. Then she realized Maia was simply waiting for her to work it out for herself.

And she did, eventually.

It came to her quietly, as she sat watching the trees, and listening to Yara's breathing. Anyone who let their heart and their feet decide was never going to give up. The music was about hope, about keeping moving forward.

'I think my mum would like you very much,' she said to Maia.

Rosa felt scared, and upset, and didn't know if the twins and Orinti would agree to it, but she knew what they had to do.

Though Yara had told them not to, it made perfect sense: she couldn't track the sloth, so they had to do it for her. Mr B. Taverner's work deserved to be completed. They couldn't simply sit back and let Professor Wiesman win.

Chapter Eighteen

Orinti had a canoe. He also owned bow and arrows, and a determination that more than matched Rosa's. He agreed to the trip immediately, as did the twins.

'We're doing this for your sister,' he said to Vita and Enzo.

'And my good friend,' Rosa added, because she owed a lot to Yara. If it hadn't been for her, she'd still be in England, feeling guilty about Opal and waiting for news from her mother.

Firstly, in order to leave the camp, a small lie had to be told. That job was given to Vita who, Rosa predicted, would be pretty convincing.

The next morning, as the sun rose above the trees, Vita told her parents that they'd changed their minds: perhaps it was time to return to Renascida, after all. What Yara needed now was peace and quiet to recover.

'Orinti's going to show us a quicker route home,' Vita said, adding, 'We might even be back in time for lessons later this morning.'

Personally, Rosa thought this last part was a bit much, but if Maia and Finn doubted her they didn't show it. Nor did the Xanti, who waved them off until the first bend in the river took them safely out of sight.

As soon as they were on their own, Enzo started to have doubts.

'We are doing the right thing, aren't we?' he asked. 'I mean, these men are pretty dangerous.'

What he said was true: the race to find the Giant Sloth had taken a darker turn. Yara might've died from that poison dart.

Vita, though, was very firm.

'Enzo,' she said, turning round and taking his face in her hands. 'There are *ants* in this jungle more dangerous than Mr Carter. And that's before we even start on the cattle men and the oil men, and all they're destroying.'

It was, Rosa thought, a very good point.

Orinti's boat was bigger and smarter than the one they'd borrowed from Josue. It was painted a bright butterfly blue, and this time each of them had a paddle. They sat two abreast: Orinti and Vita in front, Enzo and Rosa behind. What little cargo they carried – water for drinking, hard-boiled eggs, a bunch of green bananas – rolled about at their feet. Vita had also brought Yara's knapsack.

'I didn't ask *exactly*,' she admitted. 'But I'm guessing there's directions and notes and other useful stuff inside.'

They agreed to have a proper look when they stopped for lunch.

For the first half a mile or so, the river was narrow and fast-flowing. In order to keep control of the boat they used the paddles to slow their speed, reaching sideways to the bank or pushing down into the silty riverbed. There were rocks to watch out for, and vines that slithered snake-like into the water. Once, when Enzo's paddle came too close, one of the rocks moved. The caiman swam past slowly, watching them, its eyes and nostrils just visible above the water. Rosa didn't think she'd ever get used to seeing incredible sights like this.

Before long, the narrow channel met the river proper. Now the paddling began in earnest. They were travelling upstream, moving against the current. Everyone was expected to paddle, and paddle hard. Rosa was worried she wouldn't be able to keep pace with the others. Within minutes, her arms were aching, then burning, but she gritted her teeth and kept going.

What helped take her mind off the pain was thinking about how they'd track the Giant Sloth. They'd left in such a hurry this morning that no one had mentioned how they planned to go about it. Orinti was bound to have ideas, and the twins knew a lot about the jungle. It made her think back to Opal, and to Billy. In her next letter, she'd tell him how tracking wasn't about guns or beating the undergrowth with sticks – it was what Yara had told her that night when they'd first met, about being quiet and using your brain.

It also helped that the current in this part of the river wasn't especially strong. The channel was wide and slow, winding between little wooded islets and under the boughs of giant trees. They'd been travelling for an hour or more when Vita raised her hand.

'Shhhh!' She'd seen something.

Everyone stopped paddling.

'There!' she hissed, pointing to the left-hand bank, where the undergrowth was a dense, overlapping green.

The leaves moved slightly. A bird flew up, squawking in alarm, then everything settled again.

'I can't see anything,' Enzo insisted.

Rosa couldn't either, but a feeling of unease came over her. They waited a bit longer. Orinti kept very still, but soon Enzo was lifting his paddle off his knees, ready to move on.

There was movement again, this time further along the bank.

Vita tensed. 'He's still there.'

It was harder to see now the sun had climbed above the canopy. Everything beneath was in shadow. Yet where the undergrowth thinned enough to let in the light, the panama hat was easy to pick out. It was moving quickly. The cream shape flashed intermittently through the trees.

Dread grew in Rosa's stomach. She hadn't counted on two people following them. Orinti said something in his own language that sounded like a cuss.

'D'you suppose Mr Carter has invested in a new hat?' said Enzo, trying to make light of it.

'Panama Hat's the leader,' Rosa reminded him.

'He's the one giving Mr Carter orders.'

'Two of them?' Vita replied. 'Well, there's four of us.'

'On water we'll be quicker,' added Orinti.

Rosa lifted her paddle. The feel of it, solid against her palms, gave her courage.

'Let's keep moving,' she said.

With a burst of anxious speed they were soon able to put a decent distance between themselves and the man in the hat. But they stayed watchful. There was plenty else to look at too – lizards that walked on the water, river otters the size of large dogs. Dearly, Rosa would've loved to stop and take it all in, but the possibility of Mr Carter and the panama-hatted man nipped at their heels. They couldn't afford to slow down.

Thankfully, they'd found a decent paddling rhythm. The blue boat surged upstream, and as the river stayed wide and uncomplicated they were able to make good progress. So much so that, earlier than expected, Orinti declared it safe enough to stop for food and rest.

The sun was directly above them. Out on the water they felt the full force of it, but even under the trees the heat was intense. Rosa's shirt stuck to her back, her hair limp around her shoulders.

'Time for a swim,' Enzo declared.

Once Orinti had checked there weren't any caiman or dangerous eels or men in panama hats lurking, they all charged into the river fully clothed. The water was cool and soft against Rosa's hot skin. As she lay back, floating, her sore arm muscles began to unknot. Every now and then she'd feel a gentle flickering sensation as fish swam past her legs. A few yards away, the twins and Orinti were laughing and splashing each other.

This, Rosa thought, closing her eyes against the sun, *is happiness.* And she hoped it was all right to be feeling it, when so much else seemed difficult and unfair.

After swimming, they ate the hard-boiled eggs, the bananas, and picked a yellow fruit growing nearby that tasted like overripe pear. When Vita went down to the water's edge to wash her sticky hands, she lifted Yara's bag from the boat.

'Hope she's got a compass,' Rosa said.

'And some chocolate,' replied Enzo.

'We don't need either when we have this –' Orinti tapped his head – 'and this –' and gestured to the forest.

'Says the boy who got food poisoning off a *berry*!' Enzo snorted.

Orinti launched himself at Enzo. The two of them rolled about, laughing and playfighting: Vita stepped over them, tutting, to sit beside Rosa.

'*Idiota,*' she muttered as she opened the bag.

Inside was a single book, nothing else.

'Perhaps she hadn't packed yet,' suggested Rosa.

The book was called *The Extinct Amazon*, and was written by *Professor Klaus Wiesman.* Under the title was a photograph of a round-faced man with a moustache.

'At least we know what he looks like, I suppose,' said Vita.

'Hmmm.' Rosa chewed her lip. 'He's not what I was expecting.'

In her mind, the professor was bald, thin, with a straggly pointy beard and ice-cold eyes. The man on the book cover looked quite harmless – as much as you could tell from a photo.

On the flap inside the book was another picture of the same mild-looking man and, beneath it, a short paragraph about his life.

'Hang on . . . that . . . can't be . . .' She pointed to the dates next to the professor's name. She couldn't believe what she was reading.

'Boiling bananas!' Vita gasped, reading it herself.

The fighting boys sprang apart, startled.

'What's going on?' Enzo huffed, sitting up, red-faced and sweaty.

'No, that really can't be right,' Rosa said again.

'What can't be?' Enzo got to his feet.

She turned the book round to show him the paragraph.

'Read it,' she said.

Enzo's eyes skimmed the page, his expression changing as he took it all in.

Professor Klaus Wiesman, world expert on extinct species, had been killed in an aeroplane crash in 1932. It said so, on the page, in clear, bold print. Yara's rival in the search for the Giant Sloth had been dead for fourteen years.

If Professor Wiesman – the real Professor Wiesman –

didn't exist any more, then the man Mr Carter and Panama Hat were working so hard to protect was using a dead person's name. It was very mysterious – and rather sinister too.

'Why would he do that, though, pretend to be a dead man?' Enzo asked with a shiver.

'Huh! Because it makes him seem important,' decided Orinti. 'He wants to scare Yara into giving up.'

Vita shook her head. 'Yara wouldn't fall for that. She must know the real professor is dead.'

'Then why didn't she say so?' Enzo demanded.

Rosa thought for a moment.

'You know they're already using a code name – Odessa? Maybe this is another one.'

'Code names?' Enzo pulled a face. 'Whatever for?'

To Rosa it was obvious. 'Because they've got something to hide?'

What hadn't changed was their determination to keep going. There was still a Giant Sloth to find, still Yara's grandfather's project to complete. Despite not knowing who their rival was any more, they were all set on sticking to the original plan of heading north-west towards the caves.

'We're not giving up now,' Vita said, seizing her paddle like a spear.

'We'll need to be extra-careful, though,' Enzo warned. 'These people are a shady lot. Don't forget what they did to our sister.'

And don't forget we're tracking a seven-foot monster, Rosa thought to herself. Seeing a real live Giant Sloth would be the scariest thing of all.

On the next stage of the journey, the paddling felt harder. The afternoon was hot. What sun there was shone hazily, and then disappeared completely as the sky thickened with storm clouds. The heat kept building, pressing down on them so it almost felt as if there was no air left. Insects swarmed over the river's surface. Rosa quickly learned the art of paddling with her eyes down and mouth shut.

The storm arrived suddenly, as if someone had turned a switch. Within moments they were soaked, the rain coming down straight and hard, making hundreds of little ripples across the water. And not just rain – thunder too, so devastatingly loud it made Rosa cower and press her hands to her ears.

'Can't we shelter somewhere?' Enzo yelled.

'Where?' Rosa yelled back.

She'd paid enough attention in science lessons to know open water and trees were exactly the wrong places to be in a thunderstorm. They kept paddling cautiously, crouched down in the boat.

You don't know what you're getting yourself into, Yara had warned them. It certainly felt safer to keep moving.

Just as they'd passed under an overhanging branch, lightning struck it. There was a cracking sound overhead. The air smelled of burning. Rosa felt the hair on her skin lift. Then a terrific splash as the branch sheared off and fell into the river.

Up until now Orinti had been the calm one. But even he looked alarmed, and mimed fast paddling. Around the next bend in the river was a red-sand beach. The sand was wet, pocked with what Enzo said were Capybara feet. But it was safe – out of the water and out from under the trees.

By the time the storm had finally eased, it was late afternoon. Rosa was aching all over, and shivering. So when Vita suggested they stay put for the night she could've hugged her.

'I'll fish. The rest of you – find firewood.' Orinti snapped his fingers at Rosa and the twins.

An hour later, they were sitting around a fire, toasting fish on the ends of sticks. It was all down to Orinti, Rosa thought. He might be the youngest here, but he knew how to survive better than any of them. The forest was his true home. After the fish, he gave them each a root that looked like a knobbly potato. They had to chew it then spit it out onto leaves, which were then sealed up and put on the fire.

'Honestly, it's delicious,' Vita assured her.

The end result was a bit like mashed potato, only grittier, and sweeter, and tasted incredible.

After supper, Orinti offered to tell a story. The twins made enthusiastic noises before lying down, arms behind heads, as relaxed and at ease as if they were on the veranda at home. Rosa stayed sitting. She wasn't sleepy in the slightest, and was aware of little scampering noises in the forest behind them. The fire's warmth and light were very welcome, but it also made the night seem twice as dark.

She hoped this story wouldn't be as scary as the last one.

'Our tale, tonight, is of a river mermaid . . .' Orinti began.

Grateful for what sounded like a gentle story, Rosa felt her shoulders loosen.

Orinti's voice almost mimicked the quiet lapping of the river against the sand. As he explained the mermaid was a mythical creature, who could change from dolphin to human and back again, Rosa curled up next to Vita. By the time the story finished, she was on the edge of sleep. Enzo was snoring already, and Vita seemed very still. The sudden quiet, after Orinti's voice, made Rosa alert again. She sat up.

'We should take it in turns to stay awake,' she said.

Vita stretched, yawning. 'In case of Carter and that man in the hat?'

'Yes.' She didn't mention the Mapinguary, but was thinking of that too.

Orinti's head swayed slightly. He looked exhausted. Enzo snored on. Vita yawned again.

'I'll take first watch,' Rosa offered.

Soon everyone was asleep but her. As Rosa sat, prodding the flames, she thought about the last time she'd slept in the jungle, and how Vita told her she was brave. Tonight her friends were here, and it felt so much better. *She* felt so much better, despite everything.

Tipping her head back, she gazed up at the stars. There were so many patterns, so many colours, it was like watching a blizzard of light above the trees. No wonder the piece of music was called 'Stars of the Forest'. She hummed the tune under her breath. If Orinti had been awake, he might've told her how the different constellations were named after mythical creatures, each with their own gripping story. Tomorrow night she'd ask him.

Tomorrow night they'd have reached the caves.

She shivered with nervous excitement. Sir Clovis had said she wasn't flourishing at Westwood. She gave the fire another stir, still humming to herself.

Well, she was flourishing now.

Chapter Nineteen

At dawn, Orinti threw water on what remained of their fire. Then, after a quick wash in the river, they set off through the forest. The final leg of the journey was all on dry land. It was only a few miles to the caves from here, and Orinti was hopeful they'd reach them by noon. But the route was also uphill, without a definite path, and they'd be passing through forest where the locals had reported seeing giant sloth-type creatures.

Like the Xanti, they called the animal by its mythical name, the 'Mapinguary', their descriptions of a colossal beast with huge claws and reddish fur too close to that of a Giant Sloth to be anything else. Rosa remembered what she'd read in B. Taverner's notebook: the frantic scrawl, the underlined words, the total excitement that sprang off the page. No wonder Yara – and her rival – were so desperate to find what Mr Taverner had failed to track down.

'You know the Mapinguary protects the forest?' Orinti told them as they walked. 'That's its main purpose.'

'And it eats humans,' Enzo added helpfully.

'Bad humans, yes.'

'I could think of a few people who need eating,' Vita remarked.

'Me too,' Rosa agreed, thinking of Mr Carter.

The first mile was relatively easy. The leaf litter on the forest floor was soft underfoot, and they picked acai berries to eat on the way. Rosa had woken feeling quietly upbeat. She'd slept well in the end. There'd been no weird dreams, no sense that someone was watching them. Her body ached less than she'd expected, and she was getting used to the heat and humidity. They still had to find the caves, and a supposedly extinct creature, and do it all before a man using a world expert's name staked his claim. But she felt almost optimistic – certainly more than she'd felt about finding Opal.

Up ahead, Orinti had stopped. He was beckoning to the rest of the group to come and look at something on the ground. Rosa soon realized it was a pile of animal dung, so fresh there was steam coming off it.

'Peccaries,' confirmed Vita, after a quick, knowing glance at the pile.

'A type of wild pig,' Enzo explained, seeing the quizzical look on Rosa's face.

'Are they vicious?' Rosa asked.

'No,' Enzo replied. 'Giant Sloths eat them.'

'Oh!' She understood. If they were going to find a Giant Sloth they had to first find its food source. It was why Opal had made a beeline for Mrs Penwick's sheep.

Rosa felt a new, sharp thrill of excitement. This creature they were tracking wasn't just a name in an old notebook, a story told around campfires to remind children to respect the forest. It *had* existed. The Giant Sloth would have walked through this jungle, slept amongst these trees. And perhaps – *perhaps* – it still did. The very idea took her breath away.

'Watch out for flies, with your mouth open like that,' Enzo told her.

She blinked. 'Sorry.'

But she caught Vita's eye, who looked at Enzo, who grinned at Orinti, and was glad they felt it too.

Not long after the peccary droppings, something shifted. At first it was just an atmosphere – a *sense* – that Rosa put down to her imagination working overtime. But, as they walked on, the air grew cooler, smelling dank and wet, like compost. The trees seemed closer together, crowding in on them as Orinti, ten paces ahead of everyone else, tried to cut a path through the undergrowth.

When he stopped in a small clearing, beckoning to them to come quickly, Rosa felt her first pang of actual fear. She spun round, expecting to catch sight of a panama hat or a white man's face. Or maybe . . . just maybe . . . Orinti had seen something bigger.

When they caught up, he was staring at a footprint on the ground.

'Well, it's not human,' Vita said, hands on hips.

'Waaaay too big for that,' agreed Enzo.

Rosa crouched down for a closer look. The footprint wasn't shaped like a hoof-print either. There were faint toe marks, but no sign of a paw pad, which ruled out a jaguar. With her fingers, she traced the toe prints: there were three of them.

Hadn't Mr Taverner's witnesses mentioned footprints?

Rosa swallowed, her mouth dry. 'You don't think . . . ?'

'Three toes?' Vita nodded very slowly. 'Like in Orinti's story . . . ?'

'Whoa!' Enzo cried, startling birds in the overhead trees. 'We haven't found the sloth already?'

Orinti, whose dark head only reached as far as Enzo's shoulder, grabbed his arm.

'Stop making noise!' he hissed. 'If it is here, you'll scare it away!'

'Or get its attention,' Vita warned.

With a flap of his hand, Orinti ordered them to be silent. He stood very still, his face alert, eyes scanning the forest. The others watched. Waited.

They kept still for what felt like a very long time. All around them the forest squawked and crackled, sounding even louder than the thundering pulse in Rosa's ears. She caught herself thinking of Opal. This was the way to track an animal, not like she and Billy had done, stumbling noisily up a muddy lane.

Eventually, Orinti waved them on and they started walking again. They were warier now – heads turning left and right at the slightest noise. No one spoke. The mood had definitely changed; this time Rosa was sure she wasn't imagining it.

And no wonder.

A Giant Sloth might be moments ahead of them – or behind. Right at this second, it could be sniffing the air, smelling their human smell or listening to their feet as they crunched through the forest. Maybe it was tracking them, just like they were tracking it.

Rosa checked over her shoulder. No sign of anything behind. But her heart was thumping faster than ever. The Giant Sloth was aggressive. It killed people. The skeleton she'd seen at the museum was almost the size of a *Tyrannosaurus rex*. In all the stories and accounts she'd heard, it was a horrible, stinking monster.

They had good reason to be scared.

Even the forest itself felt more sinister now. The trees were darker green, their roots hunched above the ground like huge, clenching claws. Higher up, the thick canopy weakened the sunlight so everything seemed murky.

When Orinti beckoned them forward again, they crept carefully, conscious of where they were putting their feet. And, all the time, eyes open, ears strained. Every shriek of bird, every rustle of leaves made them stop and listen. When something crashed through the undergrowth to their left, Vita seized Rosa's hand.

'Shhh!' Orinti said, though no one was talking.

A noise like chattering teeth came next, then a gruff, almost dog-like bark. The leaves parted. A blur of animal rushed across their path. Rosa froze to the spot.

'Peccary!' Enzo clutched his chest.

They all breathed again.

Up ahead were more droppings, these ones bigger than the peccaries. No one was able to say which animal they'd come from. Vita suggested smelling them, and breaking them apart with sticks, which even Enzo managed to do without joking. The droppings might've been a tapir's, but no one could say for certain.

'We're close,' Enzo insisted. 'I can *feel* it.'

Rosa did too.

Not long after that, they saw the mountains for the first time. The land rose up suddenly, and dramatically, above the trees, the pale yellow rock in stark contrast to the green forest. Now, at least, they could see their destination. Another mile and the ground began to go steeply uphill. The soil grew thinner, rockier, the trees not as leafy, which meant less in the way of shade. The height of the sun suggested it was almost midday. And hot. This last bit of the journey was hard, sweaty work. Then, just as the forest gave way completely to open scrub, they discovered a whole trail of the three-toed footprints. Everyone stopped, stunned. Rosa chewed an end of damp hair.

'Cripes alive, now what?' Enzo whispered.

'These footprints lead towards the caves, so that's probably where we'll find water,' Orinti said confidently.

Vita was fanning herself with both hands. Everyone was getting tired, and thirsty. The caves weren't far away – ten minutes at most – where there would be shade and, if Orinti was right, water. And, though no one said it, they were all thinking it: they might also find a sloth.

In fact, it took less than ten minutes. A scramble over the lip of the hill, and there it was, the sheer rock face of the mountain just fifty yards ahead. The caves were dark hollows that looked like surprised mouths or startled eyes. Not all of them were at ground level: Rosa wondered if the Giant Sloth could climb. There was no sign of any life. No more footprints. No suspicious droppings. The trail had gone cold.

Rosa flopped against the nearest rock.

'Where's the water?' she asked. She'd been expecting a mountain stream, the sort you could put your face into and gulp your fill of ice-cold water.

Orinti pointed down at his feet.

'Underground springs?' She groaned. 'So we have to go through the caves?'

'Not until we're sure the Mapinguary isn't inside,' Orinti replied.

'How do we do that?'

'We call it.'

Rosa stared at him. 'You're going to call a giant, human-eating monster?'

It was the most thrilling idea she'd ever heard.

'Why not? If it charges us, we run to the nearest tree,' Orinti assured her.

The plan was dangerous. But they'd come this far. They'd got this close. And despite being so terrified her

186

legs felt like soup, Rosa was desperate to see this creature for which so many people had searched.

Wisely, though, they chose the tree first, a huge sequoia that could be reached in a few paces, and climbed relatively easily. Rosa insisted on a test run, just to be sure. It was a bit of a scramble up the trunk, especially with sweaty hands and wobbly legs, but she managed it.

After a few anxious glances, everyone agreed they were ready. Orinti cupped his hands to his mouth.

'Hang on a sec,' Enzo interrupted. 'How d'you know what a Giant Sloth sounds like?'

Orinti dropped his hands with a sigh. 'The old stories tell us.'

'Oh, okay.'

'Can I start now?'

Enzo nodded.

The sound that came from Orinti's mouth was so horrible Rosa covered her ears. No animal she knew made a noise like that. The closest thing to it was the eerie wailing they'd often heard when the air-raid sirens went off over Lancaster.

They waited. Rosa was coiled, ready to run. She scanned the horizon, the caves, the forest behind them. Nothing appeared. Orinti tried again. A few birds flew up, then settled back on the trees.

'Doesn't look like they're— Oh!' Enzo spun round.

'What on earth is that INFERNAL NOISE?' a voice boomed.

It was coming from just out of their sightline, where

the ground rose then dipped into a shallow basin.

'I travel here for peace and quiet and am met with this DISTURBANCE!' The voice was a man's, thick with a European accent.

Rosa froze. The twins looked equally startled. Orinti was already hurrying back to the cover of the forest, waving them to follow.

It was too late. The owner of the voice emerged, squinting, into the sunlight. He wasn't Mr Carter – Rosa knew this straight away – and he wasn't thin enough to be Panama Hat. But they'd been beaten here to the caves, that was obvious, which must mean this was the man using the dead professor's name.

Chapter Twenty

The man strode towards them, thumbs tucked in his belt hooks. Rosa braced herself for more yelling. It was written on his face, the outrage at being disturbed by a group of thirsty children when he was doing important scientific work.

We're here for the same reason as you! Rosa thought, hot and indignant. Though it was better not to admit it out loud, not until they'd got the measure of their rival. In her experience, what tended to work best with angry adults was either staying quiet, or being charmingly polite.

Deciding on the latter approach, she held out a hand.

'Hullo . . . Mr . . . um . . .' she hesitated, hoping desperately that the twins were standing right behind her.

To her surprise the man's face suddenly transformed. Now he was smiling down at her, like a sweet, doting grandparent.

'Professor Wiesman at your service,' he said, and bowed from the waist.

Rosa blinked.

'Professor Wiesman,' she repeated. So he was keeping up the pretence. 'Good morning, or umm . . . is it good afternoon?'

She glanced over her shoulder for Vita and Enzo, who were there, thank goodness, looking as flustered as she was. And Orinti, who'd come back when he realized they weren't following.

'Are you lost, my dears?' the professor asked, sounding genuinely concerned.

'Umm . . .' Another quick glance at the others, who'd gone silent. Rosa straightened her shoulders. 'Well, no. We're . . . umm . . . on a hike, and came looking for water.'

'Water, yes, that's right!' Enzo joined in a little too enthusiastically.

The professor pulled a handkerchief from his trouser pocket and mopped his brow. He had to be, Rosa guessed, about sixty years old, and was wearing European clothes – heavy twill breeches, a pair of black leather boots. No wonder he was sweating. Just looking at his outfit made Rosa grow hotter and thirstier by the second.

'Do you know where we can get water?' she asked. 'We've heard there are springs underground.'

There was a split second where the professor hesitated, before opening his arms as wide as a party host.

'My dears, you had better come with me. I can offer you refreshments, at the very least. Please.' He indicated they should follow him. 'Come. You are most welcome to stay for tea.'

Rosa shot a look at Vita, who was frowning, and

Orinti, who was desperately shaking his head. But the man had already set off, with Enzo following, so they had no choice but to go too.

'What are we *doing*?' Vita hissed to Rosa as they trailed behind. 'We don't know what he's up to, or his real name. I don't trust him.'

Enzo slowed down, enough to be out of earshot. 'We don't have to trust him. We just have to eat his food.'

'Huh!' Orinti glowered. '*I* can find us food!'

Rosa didn't trust the professor, either. But she guessed that by talking to him he might reveal what he knew about the Giant Sloth, and what he was up to with Mr Carter and Panama Hat.

'We'll just stay for a bit, yes?' Rosa suggested.

'I thought we were here to find a Giant Sloth, not take tea with strangers,' Vita replied reluctantly.

The professor's camp was another surprise. It consisted of three sizeable tents arranged in a circle at the base of the cliff face, in a spot that was currently blessed with shade. The effect was more of a village fête or a summer fair than a serious explorer's camp.

'Gosh!' Rosa muttered.

'Bit fancy, isn't it?' Vita agreed under her breath.

The entrance to each tent was tied open, which probably wasn't sensible given the amount of insects around. Inside the biggest of the tents, Rosa glimpsed a bookcase, a cast-iron bed, a writing desk. In the next was a drawing-room-type space with cushions, chairs and unlit lanterns hanging from the roof. The third and smallest tent was a sort of store, containing wine crates, tins of pâté, mushrooms, biscuits. Rosa even spotted the distinctive bright red of pilchard tins, Opal's favourite.

Where the tents met, the ground was covered with a huge carpet – a proper Oriental one, like there'd been on the floors at Westwood. There was also a table laid with china and silver cutlery. And on the cooking fire a copper kettle steamed. Everything had an air of luxury about it, as if a fine European house had simply been picked up, carried across the ocean and dropped here.

The truth was it would've taken ages – and many men like Mr Carter – to bring everything this far into the jungle. And getting across Europe in the first place must've been tough, with all the damaged roads and railways. Yet somehow, this man, and his possessions, had made it.

And Rosa's family hadn't. This was the part she didn't understand.

'Sit, my dears, sit!' The professor invited them to take seats at the table.

Orinti refused outright; the others sat, warily. They watched as tea was made, biscuits arranged on plates. The professor opened a tin of Genoa cake, which glistened like something slippery, and quickly attracted flies.

'Help yourselves – eat your fill,' he told them, taking only one small shortbread biscuit for himself and balancing it on his saucer.

There were lemon biscuits, chocolate biscuits, long finger-shaped ones with jam in the middle. A memory stirred in Rosa's brain, of shop windows full of biscuits just like these. But after days of eating local food they tasted too sweet. The sugar made her teeth ache. Across the table from her, Enzo cut himself more of the sticky cake. He offered a slice to Orinti, who sniffed it and shook his head. Vita sipped her tea suspiciously before downing it in one scalding gulp.

'Can we go yet?' she whispered.

'Soon,' Rosa promised, realizing they'd eaten most of the biscuits and emptied the teapot without saying a word to their host.

She wiped her mouth.

'Are you staying here long, Professor?' she asked. 'Your camp is very comfortable.'

'Isn't it?' he agreed, eyes twinkling at her over his teacup. 'I do have other business back in the city, but I might stay here a while—'

'Until you find the Giant Sloth, isn't that right?' Enzo interrupted.

Orinti breathed in sharply through his teeth.

'Enzo!' Vita wailed.

'What?' muttered Enzo. 'That's what he's here for, isn't it?'

But realizing he'd just blown any cover they had he slumped in his seat. Rosa watched the professor closely. He was still smiling at his guests, but it was a smile that didn't quite reach his eyes.

'Aha, so you know about my ambitions?' he asked. 'I confess I'm not surprised. Many people have tried before me, but I want to find a living specimen, not the remains of one – that's already been attempted, somewhat badly, by an Englishman.'

Rosa winced at the reference to Mr Taverner, whose Giant Sloth skeleton he would've seen when he visited the museum. *Bernard* Taverner, Finn's father, grandfather to the twins and Yara. Across the table, Vita was glaring at Enzo, willing him to keep quiet.

'According to the people who live here, this area is known for sightings of the Mapinguary,' Rosa said carefully.

'The—?' The professor faltered, quickly recovering himself. 'Oh yes, that's what they call it here, isn't it? My dear, is that an Austrian accent I detect?'

The sudden swerve in topic took Rosa by surprise.

'Um . . . well . . . actually . . .' She felt her face redden. She'd spoken English for so long she didn't think there was any trace of an accent in her voice.

'Are your parents *Austrian*?' The professor leaned towards her across the table. 'Are they still there? Are they happy now the war is over?'

He was interested: she wasn't sure why, and it made her suddenly lightheaded. She couldn't trust this man, and yet . . . and yet . . . he was asking about her family. No one else had even tried. All she knew of their fate was what she'd overheard behind closed doors, and even though it felt dangerous talking to a stranger about them she couldn't not seize this chance.

'I'm from Vienna,' she answered, sitting up taller in her seat. 'My mother is English, my father an Austrian.'

'Then this is why you speak English so well.'

'I've lived in England since I was three and a half. I did speak a bit of German too, and some Hebrew.'

Professor Wiesman narrowed his eyes. '*Hebrew?* So you're Jewish?'

'My father was,' Rosa explained. 'Not my mother. I don't know where any of my family are.'

'Hmm . . . intriguing.' The professor looked about to say something more, but instead stood up, brushing the crumbs from his breeches.

'About this sloth. What do you children know of it?' he asked.

Rosa frowned, confused. 'But weren't we just talking about—'

'You've seen something out here, haven't you?' he interrupted brusquely. 'You do know something. Your little friend keeps looking towards the forest.'

'That's because he's anxious to leave,' muttered Vita.

And worried about too much contact with yet another outsider, Rosa guessed.

'Ah, so you don't trust me? Despite eating all my biscuits?' The professor glared at each of them, then laughed. 'You are shrewd children. I admire your spirit.'

Vita tugged anxiously on Rosa's sleeve. 'I really think it's time to go.'

'In a minute,' Rosa hissed, wanting to return to the conversation about her family.

But their host had already started clearing the tea

things. Despite the fine-china-and-biscuits welcome, it was obvious he wanted to get rid of them. They'd been here long enough.

Enzo got to his feet. Vita did too, nudging Rosa.

'Come on,' she muttered. 'If we go now, we'll still get a few hours of searching in before sunset.'

The professor put down the tea plates.

'You know it's not uncommon for explorers to share their findings, trade information. With a search as challenging as this, it makes sense to work together,' he said, staring at Vita with new interest.

Again, Vita tugged Rosa's sleeve to go. Orinti was turning towards the forest again. They shouldn't trust this man, Rosa knew. He was working with Mr Carter, somehow, and pretending to be a dead man.

But the truth was they all wanted to find the Giant Sloth, didn't they? And maybe he had a point, that they could work together to find it. Standing there in the hot sunlight, thinking of Yara's unfinished project, it didn't seem such a terrible idea.

The professor was clearly waiting for some sort of answer, because in the end he spread his hands and sighed. 'Very well. You drive a hard bargain. Will you let me show you my evidence first?'

Four heads swung up. Four sets of eyes fixed on him.

'What evidence?' Vita asked warily.

'Cave drawings of the Giant Sloth. Here, inside these caves, on the walls.'

Rosa's stomach fluttered. She looked at Orinti, saw

the flicker of interest. Enzo – and Vita too – were both blinking in surprise.

If it was genuine, then it was a brilliant find. Admittedly, they'd not be as recent as Mr Taverner's eyewitness accounts, but they were still evidence that the Giant Sloth had lived here and people had seen it and made a record of the fact.

Vita glanced at Orinti. 'What do you think? Worth looking at?'

To someone who didn't know him, Orinti looked unimpressed. But his right leg was twitching. Enzo, more obviously, seized Vita's hand.

The professor knew then that he'd struck a deal.

After fetching a couple of lanterns from the store tent, he beckoned them to follow.

'Just a quick look and we'll go,' Rosa whispered to Vita.

'Huh! You said that about the tea,' Vita whispered back.

The professor wasn't in any hurry, ambling past the first few cave openings as if he'd all the time in the world. A short scramble up a dusty slope, and they found themselves standing at the entrance to what appeared to be quite a small cave. Next to the opening was a mechanism that looked like the pulley for raising a bucket from a well: Rosa guessed it was for drawing up water from the underground springs. The professor now lit both lanterns before reaching over Rosa, who was nearest, to hand one to Enzo. Enzo quickly passed it to Orinti as their group leader.

The entrance itself was smaller than the ones they'd already passed. The professor had to crouch down to fit through, though the children managed by dipping their heads. Immediately inside, the cave opened up into a huge, echoing cavern. The sheer walls, the rough floor were just about visible in the lantern light.

'Is it—?' Enzo went to ask something.

Professor Wiesman cut him off. 'Questions afterwards, please. This way. Straight ahead. And keep up, we don't want to lose anyone.'

At the back of the cavern was a set of steps cut roughly into the rock. These led into a passage. Though the lanterns' light quickly shrank against such total darkness, the brisk tap of the professor's leather-soled boots seemed to get louder in the smaller space. The air was stuffy, stale. They walked quickly. A bit *too* quickly: Rosa kept stumbling on the uneven ground.

Somehow, at some point, the order they were walking in changed. Orinti was now in front, the professor bringing up the rear. Out of the corner of her eye, Rosa kept catching strange shadows and peculiar shapes that made her heart beat faster. Overhead, she could almost feel the rocks squeezing down. She was beginning to realize she didn't much like being underground.

Vita touched her shoulder. 'How much further is it?'

Rosa didn't know. They'd been walking for a while now, and the passage showed no signs of ending. She didn't like it down here. And, oh, how she wished Professor Wiesman would take off his noisy boots: that incessant *tap tap tap* was making her feel worse.

The sound was like a chisel, chipping away inside her head. She tried to think of something else – swimming, stars, listening to Maia singing. But the noise seeped in, despite her covering her ears.

Tap tap tap.

The sound of feet on a staircase. Marching boots. Her horrible dream came rushing back to her, the panic pulsing through her in waves.

'I . . . think we should go back,' she stuttered.

'We have to.' Orinti held up the lantern. 'Do you see?'

Just a few yards ahead, the passage ended abruptly in a wall of bare rock. Odd that the professor hadn't called out a warning, especially as Orinti's lantern wasn't throwing out much light.

Yet the problem wasn't his candle, which still burned inside the glass. It was the fact that they now only had one lamp between them. Professor Wiesman had gone.

Chapter Twenty-one

'Should we wait for him to catch up?' asked Enzo.

'Don't be stupid,' Vita snapped. 'He's tricked us.'

'What about the cave drawings? We made a deal.'

'Enzo,' said Vita darkly, 'there probably *aren't* any cave drawings.'

Rosa was still shaking from the flashback of her dream. Nothing like it had happened before. Whatever it meant, she really didn't want to face the professor or his black boots again.

'Can't we just get out of here, and go?' she begged.

'The best idea!' Orinti agreed, and with such enthusiasm she suspected he didn't like being underground, either.

On the return leg, the passage seemed shorter. It was the relief, Rosa thought, of knowing they'd soon be out in the fresh air.

Yet, back in the cavern, another shock awaited them.

'Oh no,' wailed Rosa when she realized there was no daylight where there should've been. 'No, no, *no!*'

Apart from their lantern, the only light was the thin,

gold line running along the underside of the entrance.

'He's closed it up!' cried Vita. 'That nasty piece of work – he's shut us in!'

Orinti said nothing: he didn't need to. He'd been right all along not to trust the professor. Rosa felt guilty – and stupid – for thinking they might be able to work with the man. What on earth had she thought they could achieve?

'This isn't fair play!' Enzo cried, at last realizing the enormity of what had happened. 'If we're shut in here, he's going to find the beast first, isn't he? This is cheating!'

The door across the entrance was solid metal. Enzo drumming his fists against it made a lot of noise, but the door itself didn't move. Nor did anyone on the other side of it reply.

'Open the door!' Vita yelled. 'This is false imprisonment! What you're doing is illegal!'

When there was no answer, Rosa had a go.

'Let us out, please,' she begged. 'We won't look for the Giant Sloth any more, we'll go straight home, I promise. Just let us go.'

Rosa pressed her ear against the door. She heard movement, the scuffle of feet on dry ground. A beep, a hissing sound, like a radio being connected.

'He *is* out there! He's using a radio, I think,' she said, beckoning to the others to come and listen.

They crouched next to the door. The professor was too far away to hear every word he was saying, but he sounded totally furious:

'I've had to activate Plan B . . . Yes, I'm very aware what Plan B . . . my hiding place, in case . . . What? Well, what else could I do with a bunch of nosy kids? . . . Yes, B for Bunker! *Guter schmerz,* where did they find you?'

Then a click as the radio cut out.

All four children thumped the door at once. When they stopped and listened again, the only noise was the hush of afternoon rain.

'He's gone,' Rosa said, her heart sinking. 'Now what do we do?'

'We wait. See if he comes back,' Vita replied.

It wasn't much of a solution. Even if the professor did come back, Rosa couldn't imagine him letting them go. He and his people had already poisoned Yara, and now he'd tricked them by trapping them in a cave. The fake name, the lavish camp – there was something very wrong with it all.

Yara's warning echoed in her head: *You don't know what you're getting yourself into.* Rosa sat on the floor and hugged her knees, wishing she'd listened.

Time dragged. The twins distracted themselves with various silly games that only they knew how to play. Rosa chewed the end of her plait, feeling defeated. She could kick herself for thinking the mechanism near the entrance was for drawing water buckets. The professor had deliberately set up the door to drop like a trap. But he'd also said on the radio that the cave was *his* hiding place: from *what*, exactly? The Giant Sloth? Was it another sign that the creatures probably *did* still exist?

After what felt like ages, they tried the door again. But the same routine of thumping, yelling, cajoling was met with the same response: silence. Outside, the rain appeared to have stopped. The sunlight under the door had shifted a few degrees, signalling the afternoon was almost over. At the thought of being stuck in here all night, Rosa's frustration grew.

'We're going to have to find another way out,' she decided.

Enzo groaned.

Orinti held up the lantern. 'There's an hour's burning time left on the candle. So, if we do it, we do it now.'

It was enough to spur everyone into action.

First, they checked the cavern for alternative ways out, but the only exit was via the steps at the back of the cave. Rosa wasn't sure what Vita was doing when she dropped to her knees to thump the first step.

Nothing happened.

'Argghh!' She sat back. 'I read in a book once about a house with secret doors in the panelling and you had to knock like this—'

She did it again, harder this time. Amazingly, the stone slid backwards, making an awful grinding sound.

Vita grinned. 'Told you!'

Rosa gasped in astonishment. Where the step had been was now an opening, about the size of a narrow window.

'What's down there?' Enzo asked. 'Orinti, can you have a look with the light?'

Warily, the young boy eased the lantern through the

gap, then his arm, then his head, and finally the top of his shoulders.

'A rope ladder,' he told them when he emerged again. 'It goes down into a room, with . . .' He gestured with his free hand. 'Things.'

'What sort of things? The cave drawings?'

'No, it's a box.'

Rosa held out her hand for the light. 'Can I see, please?'

Holding the lantern aloft, she peered all the way down into what appeared to be a circular room. The box Orinti had seen was, in fact, a large suitcase. What interested her more were the multiple entrances leading off the room to goodness knew where. It had to be worth a try.

'Shall I go down?' Orinti offered, though he didn't sound very keen.

Rosa felt a pang of sympathy. The space looked even smaller and darker than the tunnel.

'Shouldn't we all stick together?' she suggested.

The twins agreed.

Since Rosa already had the lantern, she offered to go first. The drop was about twenty feet, the ladder swayed horribly and trying to grip on with one hand was so difficult that in the end she held the lantern in her teeth. It was easier for the others, thankfully, who climbed down into the light.

'Which way now?' asked Enzo.

There were three exits leading off the round room. The room itself was even smaller now they were all standing in it, shoulder squashed against shoulder. Rosa had already bashed her shin twice on the suitcase.

'I bet it's the professor's,' she said, giving the case a spiteful kick.

'But he's *not* the professor, is he?' Enzo pointed out.

She glared at the suitcase. 'I'm going to have a look inside.'

'Do it,' Vita urged. 'See if it tells us anything.'

Handing the lantern back to Orinti, Rosa dropped to her knees. She half expected the case to be locked, but the latches readily pinged open. She lifted the lid to find a thin layer of tissue paper. Underneath was an army uniform, folded immaculately, smelling faintly of cigars. Rosa recognized the grey cloth, the black collar and epaulettes on the shoulders, the eagle-shaped badge sewn on the upper arm. There was also a peaked cap bearing the same eagle badge, and a silver emblem that caught the light, glinting.

'He's a –' she swallowed – 'a Nazi.'

On one of the very few occasions at Westwood when she'd got to the newspapers before Lady Prue, she'd seen a photo of a captured Nazi officer, wearing a uniform like this one.

'It's the uniform of Third Reich – an officer, I think,' she said, her voice shaking.

'So really he's a *soldier*?' Vita asked.

'Isn't he a bit old for that?' said Enzo.

Vita tutted at her brother. 'He wouldn't have been running about with a gun, *idiota*. He'd have been one of the ones making decisions.'

Which made it worse, somehow.

Rosa didn't know what to say. This was a man who'd served in an army that believed people like her own father had no right to exist. It was because of the Nazis she'd had to leave Vienna, and had lost all contact with the only family she had left.

When she glanced up at her friends, their kind faces gazed down at her. They didn't know that much about the war, did they? Living here, it hadn't touched their lives the way it had ripped through hers. The Xanti faced their own battle against the oil companies and the cattle ranchers, and that was terrible too. But the twins had grown up quite happily with their big, difficult, fascinating family. And Rosa envied them so much she could hardly bear it. But it was too much to try to explain all in one go.

'What's that?' Vita pointed into the suitcase. 'There. Can we see it?'

Tucked in between the clothes was a book – a brand-new one, by the look of its glossy cover. As Rosa picked it up, Orinti moved closer with the lantern so they could all see it better.

The title of the book was *Unexplained Beasts of the World*, and it seemed to be aimed at children. Inside, the book was split into sections: one on the Bigfoot myth of the Rockies, another on the Himalayan Yeti, and a third on the Mapinguary (or Giant Sloth) of the Amazon. There were pictures of a creature that looked more like a giant bear, and a short paragraph on some cave drawings that had been found by an explorer in Victorian times, though it didn't say exactly where.

'Why's he carrying a kids' book?' Enzo asked. 'Isn't he a world expert?'

Rosa snorted. 'I bet you *that's* how he learned about the sloth!'

Vita gasped. 'The sly old dog! So he's not a sloth expert, either? Even that part was a lie?'

'There aren't any cave drawings, are there? He just took them straight out of this book!' Enzo cried, exasperated.

It took a moment to sink in.

'We've been really stupid, haven't we?' Orinti said miserably.

No one answered. The mood in the tiny dark chamber felt suddenly heavy and suffocating, but Rosa wasn't about to give up.

'He said he had other business in the city,' she reminded them. 'So I don't think he's planning on camping out here for long.'

Rummaging through the rest of the suitcase, she quickly found letters and a passport. The passport wasn't German issued, but was stamped with a red cross. Inside, was a photo of the professor without his beard. And in typed letters:

Herr Amon Eisenhoff.

'"Herr" means "Mr" in German,' Rosa explained.

Vita nodded. 'I'd guessed that much.'

There was no mention of him being a professor of anything. The ink was badly smudged, the document made of thin, cheap cardboard. Rosa suspected the passport wasn't genuine.

She opened the first of the letters.

Her German was basic, and very rusty – a three-and-a-half-year-old's German. But there were words on the page she recognized: times of his ship's arrival at Manaus, the name of Luella's museum. Mr Carter was also mentioned, and the codename 'Odessa'. This, though alarming, confirmed what they already knew.

'Why is he here if he's not searching for the sloth?' Enzo asked.

Right at the bottom of the page in tiny print was the name 'SHL Petrochemicals'.

'That'll be something to do with oil,' Enzo said with a groan.

'He's a bad man,' agreed Orinti. 'His fruit cake smelled of evil.'

But it was his boots Rosa was hearing again. The tap of them. The creak of leather. And not just in her dream. Hundreds of boots stomping across the cobbled square where they lived.

It was coming back to her so fast now that she had to hold her head in her hands.

They'd been indoors. The apartment was warm and smelled of soup. Liesel, hearing a noise outside, took her out onto the balcony to see what was happening. There were soldiers everywhere. The little bakery on the corner was on fire. She could smell burning and, almost as loud as the boots, the shouts, the breaking glass.

'Rosa?' Vita crouched beside her, peering into her face. 'Are you all right?'

Rosa shut her eyes. She took a deep breath. This was what Maia meant about memories and being ready. Some things you shut away until you were strong enough to remember them.

When Rosa opened her eyes again, it was as if a veil had cleared. The empty ache for her family was now pure, solid anger.

'That man we drank coffee with has done terrible things,' she said quietly.

She couldn't take it all in.

'They're arresting the Nazis and putting them on trial in Europe, aren't they?' Vita asked. 'I'm sure Minty mentioned it.'

'That's why he's really here, isn't it? He's on the run!' gasped Enzo.

Rosa glanced at Vita, who looked at Orinti, who shrugged a shoulder.

'He brought many things here to the jungle. Someone must've helped him.'

'Mr Carter,' said Vita and Rosa at the same time.

'But if he's not a sloth hunter then Yara's got no competition, has she?' Enzo tried to be optimistic. 'She'll still be the first to find the beast.'

Yet it didn't add up. Yara must've known that the real Professor Wiesman was dead. So why had she spun them all a completely compelling and convincing story? Everyone, from Sir Clovis at Westwood, to Minty at

Renascida, and Maia, her own mother, believed she was on the trail of the creature her grandfather had failed to find.

'We should move on,' Orinti warned, holding up the lantern to show them the spluttering flame. 'The light won't last.'

The uniform went back into the suitcase, but Rosa kept the papers.

'Evidence,' she said, stuffing them in the waistband of her trousers, 'that we found our monster.'

Chapter Twenty-two

Just as they'd decided which of the three entrances to try first, the flame hissed, then flattened. The candle went out. It was darker than the jungle at night. Darker than winter evenings at Westwood with the blackout curtains closed.

'We'll have to feel our way out,' Vita said confidently.

'Absolutely,' agreed Rosa, trying to copy her upbeat tone. 'We'll go slowly and keep hold of each other. We can do that, can't we?'

There was an uncomfortable pause. Everyone was anxious. Rosa could hear it in their rapid breathing. But just because they were scared didn't mean they couldn't do it. They had to get out. There were people back at the Xanti camp who'd be worried about them. The papers tucked in Rosa's trousers were another reason: she was going to report Herr Eisenhoff for being a war criminal on the run.

Meanwhile, faced with three potential exits, and no way of seeing anything, they had to try each in turn. Enzo found the nearest one by stumbling backwards into it with a startled cry. It was safer, they decided, to link hands so they wouldn't lose each other. The general feeling was to hurry, but they needed to be careful – and not just of where they were putting their feet. There was a chance Herr Eisenhoff had checked the cave, and now knew they were missing. The last thing anyone wanted was to meet him in one of these dark tunnels.

Slowly, they began to inch forward. Orinti, as was customary, was in front.

But, only a few yards in, he banged his head.

'Yeouch!' he yelped.

Feeling the rock above him, he refused to go on.

'It's too narrow,' he insisted. 'Like being buried alive.'

To everyone's surprise, his voice cracked and he started to cry. Rosa, who was right behind him, took his hand again. It felt hot and impossibly small. But he *was* small, the youngest here. For all his leading them through the forest, his stories, his knowledge, he was also a boy who got frightened. And that was all right too.

'We'll be as fine as the finest sugar,' Rosa told him. It was what Liesel used to say to her when she'd been scared, and she liked how big-sisterly it sounded.

For the next exit, they shuffled clockwise until Enzo found the opening, this time in a less dramatic fashion. The tunnel was bigger, but dipped up and down so much that holding hands became impossible.

'How will I know you're still there?' Orinti fretted.

'We could talk?' Vita suggested.

'Or sing.' Rosa hummed the first bars of 'Stars of the Forest'. It didn't sound quite as lovely as when Maia sang it, but nor was it as awful as Yara's attempt, which was something.

Vita recognized the tune. 'Our mother sings that song.'

'So does mine. She's a music teacher,' Rosa replied.

It felt odd to say it – odd but nice – as if it made her mother seem more real. *I should talk about her more often*, Rosa thought. *Especially to my friends*.

She and Vita picked up the tune, and were humming together, when Enzo told them, quite sharply, to stop. A shower of soil fell on them from above. Instinctively, Rosa's arms went up to cover her head.

'We need to go back – it's not safe!' Enzo yelled.

Stumbling, feeling the rock, they hurried back the way they'd come. They reached the little round room just in time. Deep from inside the tunnel came a rumbling. More soil fell from the roof. Then a thunder of rocks, the blast throwing them off their feet.

No one was hurt. But it meant mouthfuls of dust, a good deal of coughing and now there was only one way out left to try.

'Rosa!' Orinti found her in the dark. 'Promise you'll walk with me.'

She took his hand again. 'I will.'

At first, the final tunnel seemed the most inviting. This time Vita took the lead, and they walked in a chain, holding hands without too much stooping or banging of heads. It didn't last. There came a point where they

213

had to drop to their hands and knees start crawling. After a hundred yards or so, the tunnel dipped dramatically downhill.

'Rosa!' Orinti wailed.

He was just in front of her. She knew he'd stopped because her fingertips brushed against the soles of his feet.

'I'm here,' she told him. 'Listen to me. I'm right behind you.'

She started to sing again. The tune echoed down the tunnel. It sounded a little lost at first, like singing in an empty church. Then, barely louder than a whisper, Orinti joined in, then Enzo, in his booming, slightly tuneless way, and finally Vita. Once they got to the end of the song, they started again, Rosa keeping everyone at the right speed. They couldn't see each other or touch – the song was the thread that connected them, holding them all together.

Now and again, despite the song, Rosa's chest would tighten in fear. The tunnel was airless. Her mouth and throat felt dry. She'd think of the dead-end Herr Eisenhoff had herded them towards, and was terrified of it happening again. What would they do if this tunnel went nowhere? Crawl backwards up the slope? Scream?

Suddenly, Vita stopped singing.

'Are you okay down there?' Rosa called.

Vita didn't answer.

Worried, Rosa crawled faster, urging Orinti to do the same. Ahead, someone grunted: it sounded like Vita.

'Can't you hurry up a bit?' Rosa urged, but Orinti had slowed right down.

'Smell the air,' he said.

She hadn't noticed until then: but he was right, it did smell different – of dampness and soil. Even more thrilling was the faint grey light seeping into the tunnel. The whole space seemed to expand.

'Is this it? Have we reached the surface?'

She was talking to herself. Now that there was room to stand, Orinti was on his feet and running.

'Wait for me!' she cried.

She found the twins and Orinti just round the corner, standing in a huddle in another huge cavern. This one was deep rather than wide. And damp. Rosa could smell water. She could hear it too, a faint burbling that came from under their feet. At first glance, the walls appeared slimy and green, like the rocks near a waterfall.

The big smiles on everyone's faces told her they'd also found a way out. There was a moment of laughter. Hugs. An arm punch from Enzo.

'I told you we'd be all right,' he said, though Rosa couldn't remember if he had.

The exit was through a hole in the roof. Though glad to see the sky again, Rosa couldn't help but notice how pale it looked. Soon it would be dark, and she'd had enough of darkness.

'How do we get up there?' she asked. The hole was a considerable height above them.

'By using those.' Orinti pointed at the thick vines

curled around the lip of the hole. Some of the bigger ones grew downwards, and looked as if they might be strong enough to hold a person's weight.

Meanwhile, above them, the light was fading fast. Orinti, who was back to his practical, confident self again, located the spring and insisted, before anything else, they all drink from it. Certainly Rosa felt better for water, and for washing the dust from her eyes and nose and ears.

To test the strength of the hanging vines, Orinti went first. He selected a fat-looking specimen and shimmied up at amazing speed. At the top, in the fresh air, he waved and did a little dance.

'All right, show off.' Enzo grinned. 'I'll go next.'

Up he went, slower, the vine creaking a bit. But he made it and threw an arm round his friend's shoulders.

Next was Vita, who chose a fresh vine and, quick as a cat, climbed up it. On reaching the top, she crouched over the edge to shout encouragement down to Rosa.

'You'll be fine. Just go as quick as you can – it's easier that way. And don't look down.'

It wasn't heights that scared Rosa: it was having enough strength in her arms and legs.

'You'll pull up me if I get stuck?' she called.

'Course, don't worry.'

Rosa checked her waistband. Good, Herr Eisenhoff's papers were still there. She flicked her plaits over her shoulders. She was ready.

Climbing the vine wasn't too tricky at first. The vine itself was knotty and rough, which gave it purchase against her hands. And she tried her best to push with her legs as well as heave with her arms, as she'd watched Vita do. Of course, Vita didn't grunt or get all hot in the face. Still, Rosa had made it almost three-quarters of the way up when her legs went to jelly and refused to push any more.

'I need to stop a sec!' she panted.

Stopping made it worse. As she clung on, the vine began to turn, first one way, then another. It made her dizzy. Looking up didn't help, either, not with three silhouetted heads peering over the edge at her.

'You need to start moving again,' Vita told her.

'Or your legs will seize up and you'll be stuck there,' Enzo added.

'Bugs alive! Don't tell her *that*!' cried Vita.

Rosa tried to pull. Tried to push. The effort made her shake; she couldn't manage it.

'Use the wall,' Orinti suggested.

As the vine did another of its slow turns, she kicked out with her feet. She caught the wall oddly, scuffing a chunk of moss with her feet. The moss peeled away, thudding against rocks below her.

'Try again! Get your feet on the wall and walk up it,' Orinti told her.

'I *am* trying,' she muttered, feeling the sweat drip down her back.

This time her feet landed squarely. She steadied herself. With something solid to push against, her legs felt stronger. Rosa began to move.

As she did so, her eyes snagged on the place where the moss had ripped free. A huge clump, still attached by its roots, dangled from the rock. The stone underneath, now exposed, had marks on it. Brown splodges that she quickly realized were shapes. Faint though they were, amongst the dust and dirt, there was no mistaking the tall, bear-like body, the small head. From the short, raised front legs three claws had been drawn.

'Hey!' Rosa called, heart in throat. 'I think I've found something!'

The others were close enough to lean down and see the ancient drawings for themselves.

'Smoking toads!' Enzo gasped.

'Smoking *Mapinguary*,' Orinti corrected him.

For a long, quiet moment they stared at the pictures. It was incredible to think that, many, many years ago, someone had been where they were now, painting onto the rock face. They must've encountered a Giant Sloth – how else could they paint one so accurately?

'I wonder why they chose the sloth, and not – I don't know – a jaguar?' Rosa murmured, thinking out loud.

'To warn people to respect the forest? Like in Orinti's stories?' suggested Enzo.

'Or to look at?' said Orinti. 'The pictures are very beautiful.'

Vita grinned. 'At least we can all say we've *seen* a Giant Sloth.'

'Hmmm.' Enzo considered it. 'D'you think that Nazi man *did* know the drawings are here?'

'Huh! I doubt it,' replied Vita. 'He probably read the bit in that book and made up the rest. He's lied about everything else, hasn't he?'

'Then he's an idiot,' Enzo said vigorously. 'It's obvious we're in Giant Sloth territory. The footprints, those droppings we found earlier—'

'Were probably from a tapir,' Orinti admitted.

'All right,' Enzo huffed, a bit disappointed. 'But it *did* exist in this area.'

'Your grandfather thought so. He spoke to people who'd seen it,' Rosa said, flexing her legs. 'Though can we talk about this in a sec? I'm struggling to hold on here.'

Quickly, with one hand, she did her best to cover the drawings again with what was left of the moss. She gripped the vine. With a final burst of strength, she reached the surface. Hands grabbed her arms, her clothing, pulling her up the last few inches and over the edge. She lay, gasping, face down on the ground. When she rolled over, the stars were already out and glittering.

'Can you sit up, Rosa?' Vita's voice had changed. It sounded tight, afraid. 'We've got a bit of a problem.'

It was then Rosa realized there were four people staring down at her, when moments ago there'd been only three.

Chapter Twenty-three

Mr Carter grabbed her by the shirt collar.

'Grovelling won't help. Get up!' he hissed, hauling her to her feet.

Rosa swayed a little, dazed. Her friends were being very quiet. Then she saw why: Mr Carter was carrying an arm-length blowpipe, like the Xanti used for hunting food. Attached to his belt was a leather pouch of darts.

'No funny business,' Mr Carter warned her. 'Or you'll end up like Dr Fielding.'

The threat didn't sink in. Ducking her head, Rosa managed to twist free. She stared at him, still more angry than scared.

'You've been following us, haven't you?' she blurted out.

'It's my job to,' he said bluntly. 'So I'd behave myself if I was you.'

'And you hurt Yara!'

'Dr Fielding?' Mr Carter's hand moved to the pouch of darts. 'Sorry about that, but she was getting in the way.'

Horrified, Rosa glanced at the others. Enzo had gone pale, Vita was scowling silently and Orinti was holding his mouth shut with his fingers in the hope she'd stop talking.

'That's right – take a leaf out of your friends' book and be quiet,' Mr Carter advised. 'What's going on here doesn't concern you.'

But Rosa had been told this once too often in her life. It was like Lady Prue with her newspapers, and what she'd overheard that night at Renascida. This *did* concern her. They were trying to find the sloth to help Yara, and, even if it was dangerous and difficult, she wasn't going to stop because Mr Carter told her to do so.

'What was Yara getting in the way of?' she asked. 'The man you're working for isn't even looking for the Giant Sloth.'

Mr Carter rocked back on his heels, considering what she'd just said.

'Think you're smart, do you, working all this out? Then you'll know your Dr Fielding isn't out here searching for sloths, either.'

Rosa frowned. 'What?'

'Oh! So you *don't* know about her?' Mr Carter laughed, clearly delighted.

'Of course we do,' insisted Rosa.

But she could feel herself getting flustered. When she glanced at the twins and Orinti, they seemed as confused as she was.

'She'll have told you then, no doubt, that she's a secret

agent, working for the Allies in Europe?' He grinned horribly. 'Yes, of course you knew that.'

Rosa's ears were ringing. She felt suddenly, unbearably hot.

Yara, a secret agent?

'What *total* nonsense!' Vita snorted.

'It's just more lies,' Rosa agreed firmly.

'He's saying it to rattle us, isn't he?' Enzo said, then looked at Vita. '*Isn't* he?'

'Am I?' Mr Carter's face was strangely greasy in the twilight.

Vita raised her chin. 'We know why Yara's here, Mr Carter. She's finishing our grandfather's project.'

'Aha! But did she tell you *which* grandfather's project?'

Vita stared at him. At Enzo.

'What are you *talking* about?' she demanded.

Mr Carter pressed his fingers to his lips, smiling. He looked so different from the dishevelled, down-on-his-luck man Rosa had first met at Manaus harbour. She wasn't sure which version of him she disliked the most.

'You thought this was about Bernard Taverner, didn't you?' he asked.

It was exactly what they'd thought, and Rosa hated that Mr Carter knew as much.

'It's all sour grapes, of course. She's simply digging up an old argument. But then she always was a nosy young woman. That's why she's so good at sniffing out ratlines.'

'What's a ratline?' Enzo whispered.

Rosa had never heard the word before, either.

'Another thing you don't know!' smirked Mr Carter. 'Ratlines are what we call the escape routes we've been arranging for our Nazi comrades, so they can leave Europe. Things are going well, despite your annoyingly persistent sister.'

All this time, Orinti had kept quiet.

Now, suddenly, he rushed at Mr Carter. He hit him at speed, grabbing him around the middle. The surprise attack almost worked. Mr Carter staggered backwards. There was a flurry of elbows. A scratching of feet trying to steady themselves on the path.

Yet despite Orinti's speed, Mr Carter was too solid. The whole thing was over in seconds. When they pulled apart, Mr Carter was holding a handful of darts. He pushed one into the pipe, threatening Orinti. Red in the face, hair flopping forward, he barked at them all to start walking. They did as he asked, but only because he had an uncanny knack for training his dart on all four of them at the same time.

They marched down the side of the mountain in single file, Mr Carter and his blowpipe at the rear.

'I don't believe it,' Enzo kept muttering until a prod from Mr Carter shut him up.

The thing was, Rosa *could* see Yara as a secret agent. In the short time she'd known her, Yara had been determined, quick-thinking, got things done without drawing attention to herself. And it fitted with the story of Professor Wiesman. But to find out like this – if it *was* true – was a shock, especially for the twins. It didn't help

223

that Mr Carter was being so oily and smug about it. But Rosa's anger, now cooling, was rapidly turning to nerves. As the lush vegetation around them became dry scrub again, she guessed where he was taking them. This time there wouldn't be tea and biscuits. This time they were dealing with a Nazi.

Herr Eisenhoff's tent was tucked away between two gullies at the base of the mountain. Seen from this angle, it was a good hiding place, though at night, with candles blazing, the tents glowed like exotic lanterns.

They were met by the sound of music playing. It was coming from an old wind-up gramophone, perched on the table where earlier they'd taken their tea. The music was loud, brash, with thundering drums and crashing cymbals. Orinti covered his ears, grimacing.

The music made the hairs on Rosa's arms prickle. It was exactly the sort of music people marched to, wearing grey uniforms, and waving huge flags of red, white and black. She could picture it because she'd seen a march like this in the streets of Vienna. Just a glimpse, that was all, before Liesel pulled her away from the window, closed the shutters and turned the radio up loud to drown out the noise.

By the time they reached the table, her legs were shaking. Mr Carter made them stand in a line, deafeningly close to the music. Set on the ground around them, more lanterns blazed. The light was too bright to look at, but too dark when you looked away. It was why, at first, Rosa didn't notice Herr Eisenhoff himself, sitting at the table. It was only when a hand reached out to lift the needle off the record that her relief at the music ending turned, in half a beat, back to fear.

'Well, well, I wasn't expecting to see you all again – and so soon,' Herr Eisenhoff said, sounding bored. 'How charming.'

He was eating what smelled like tinned fish. The whole arrangement was ridiculous – snowy white tablecloth, napkin stuffed down his collar, wine, crystal glasses, bone china plates – and all for a supper that at best reminded Rosa of what she'd fed to Opal.

'You tricked us.' This time, Vita was the first to speak.

Shoulders back, chin up, she was as brave as she'd been the night Rosa met her. Though Herr Eisenhoff, who carried on eating, didn't seem impressed.

'And you, my dears, were stupid enough to fall for it,' he replied, his mouth full of fish.

'Now, look here.' Enzo tried to be reasonable. 'Why don't we leave you in peace to eat your supper, and we'll go home and forget—'

Herr Eisenhoff laughed. 'Ha! I don't think so!'

'You can't keep us here!' Vita cried. 'We're not prisoners!'

'True, I wouldn't use that word, either, but I can't let you go. It's far too risky.'

Rosa clenched her jaw. She was trying hard not to shake, or to say something that would only make things worse. This man was different from Mr Carter. He was in charge, for one thing. And where Mr Carter was smug, Herr

Eisenhoff was ruthlessly cool. They had to tread carefully if they were going to persuade him to let them go.

But Orinti was getting restless. Under his breath, he muttered that he'd had enough of being told what to do by 'this stinky-fish-eating man' and was heading back to his canoe.

'Not yet!' Vita hissed, grabbing his arm.

The sudden movement caught Herr Eisenhoff's eye. For the first time, he looked almost interested.

'Go on, boy, run. You won't get far. Mr Carter, for all his stupidity, is a very good shot.'

Mr Carter grunted, not sure how to take the remark.

'I would like to let you go,' Herr Eisenhoff continued. 'I'll be honest, I'm not very fond of children, and you four are particularly tiresome. But I know who you are and your links to Dr Yara Fielding, so . . .' He shrugged.

'And we know who you are, Mr Nazi Oil Man,' Orinti spat.

Sweat prickled between Rosa's shoulder blades. Enzo rubbed his face in his hands, realizing the situation was heading in the wrong direction, though for once it wasn't his doing.

'Why did he have to go and say that?' he whispered.

Rosa wondered why Herr Eisenhoff was still eating pilchards, still smiling. Then she felt Mr Carter barge past, and, turning, saw him grab Orinti roughly by his arms.

'Hey!' she cried. 'Let go of him!'

'You're next!' Mr Carter growled, and tried to trip her with his leg.

As she jumped back, something fell from her waistband. She felt it, sliding down the leg of her trousers, before realizing what it was. By the time she did, Herr Eisenhoff had seen it too. The fork paused, halfway to his mouth.

He was on his feet, chair flung back, glasses tumbling. Rosa wasn't quick enough. He swept the table aside and flew at her. The force of it almost knocked her over. But he had her hair and yanked her upright by it, the pain making her yelp.

His other arm was crushed against her chest. Something cold, sharp – the fork she guessed – was pressing against her throat.

'Give me that passport,' he said quietly. 'I know you're standing on it.'

Rosa winced. His breath smelled of wine and pilchards.

'And any other papers you stole,' he added.

When she didn't move, he pressed harder on the fork.

'Do it, Rosa,' Vita pleaded.

The twins were being guarded by Mr Carter. There was no way she could pass the papers to them.

Where was Orinti?

She couldn't see him at all.

'Oh dear, I seem to be waiting,' Herr Eisenhoff said. 'And, do you know, I really don't enjoy being made to wait. I find it *very* dull.'

He yawned against the side of her face. When she tried to turn away from his horrid breath, he yanked her hair again, hard.

'Make your mind up, *kinder*,' he hissed in her ear.

Rosa tried to think. Did she really need the papers to prove who he was? If she gave him what he wanted, would he actually let them go?

'You've got five seconds to hand everything over,' Herr Eisenhoff decided. 'Five, four—'

'They're back in the cave! She dropped them!' Enzo cried.

'Nice try.' Herr Eisenhoff smiled sweetly at him. 'Three, two—'

'Rosa!' Vita begged. 'Just give him the papers.'

'One—'

Chapter Twenty-four

Rosa would've picked the papers up. She was about to do it, right then, when the animals came out of the darkness. Slowly, silkily: two beautiful adult jaguars – one black, one spotted. They made no noise. And, for a second, Mr Carter wasn't aware of them. Nor were the twins.

But Herr Eisenhoff saw them at the same time as Rosa. He dropped his fork. It landed at Rosa's feet, and with a swift sweep of her left foot, she pushed it out of reach. The papers went with it.

The cats approached the dinner table, sniffing the air. They were in full view of everyone now. The twins knew exactly how to behave, and kept still. But Herr Eisenhoff, who still had Rosa by the hair, started to panic.

'Shoot them,' he ordered, which, since he was the only person with a weapon, was directed at Mr Carter.

Rosa's heart plummeted. It was always the answer, wasn't it, for people like Herr Eisenhoff? Shoot the dangerous animal. Get rid of what we don't understand. The jaguars were curious – that was all. What did the man expect, eating pilchards out in the open? This was their jungle, not his.

'They'll go in a minute if we're quiet,' Rosa tried to tell him.

'I didn't ask for your advice,' Herr Eisenhoff snapped.

But he did at least try to stay still. The spotted jaguar, a magnificent male, crawled under the table where some of the food lay scattered. The female leapt up onto it and, finding bits of unfinished supper splattered across the tablecloth, began licking at it. She was so close Rosa could hear the rasp of her tongue against the cloth. For one magical moment, her mind emptied of marching boots, Mapinguarys, and Nazi passports.

Oh, Billy, she caught herself thinking. *If only you could see this!*

When the black jaguar lifted her head, she looked straight at Rosa and Herr Eisenhoff. Her tail thumped against the table, her whiskers began to shiver, her lips curled back from her teeth. Whether she'd smelled more pilchards or Herr Eisenhoff's fear, Rosa didn't know. But he'd seen the change in the cat too. He stumbled back just as the creature leapt.

The table flipped over, and there was a flash of spotted fur as the male jaguar bolted out from underneath. Everyone was moving all at once: Mr Carter taking aim. The twins trying to stop him. Rosa throwing herself sideways out of the way as the female cat collided with Herr Eisenhoff, hitting him in the chest. Already stumbling, he fell backwards into the tent.

'Arrghhhh! Get it off me! Someone shoot it!' he screamed.

Mr Carter rushed into the tent. It was enough to scare the jaguar. She bolted from the tent, past Rosa, and was gone. The twins, who'd been clinging to each other, finally stepped apart. Vita went to Rosa, grabbing her hand.

'We've got to go, quickly – this is our chance,' she cried, nodding in the direction of the tent from where groaning could be heard.

The shadows of Herr Eisenhoff sitting up and Mr Carter crouching next to him loomed against the canvas. By the time the authorities had been alerted and traced the runaway Nazi, he would've packed up camp and be long gone, another ratline opening up for him.

'But his papers!' Rosa groaned, looking around frantically.

The ground was littered with broken plates, upturned chairs, cutlery and glass. She'd never find the passport amongst this lot.

'And where's Orinti?' she cried. 'We can't leave without him.'

'He'll have gone on ahead. Now *come on*!' Vita urged.

Just then the tent began to sway. Next came a crumpling sound as the canvas sagged at the back. Then an awkward lurch and the sides went down too. Caught underneath it were the oblongs of a bed and a desk and two men fighting their way out.

'Hey!' Mr Carter's muffled voice could be heard. 'What's going on? If you little bleeders have done this . . .'

And there was Orinti, emerging from behind the tent. He was clutching an armful of tent pegs, and wearing a very big grin.

'You genius!' Enzo cried.

'Not quite yet,' he cautioned, and told them all to take a guy rope each.

As the men underneath shouted and swore and wriggled, they criss-crossed the ropes over the canvas. By the time they'd finished the men were trussed up like an enormous, angry parcel.

'Wait till I get my hands on you!' bellowed Mr Carter.

'You *ROTZLÖFFELS*!' Herr Eisenhoff roared.

Recognizing the German word, Rosa couldn't help smiling. '"*Snot spoons*", that's what he's just called us.'

Enzo had the look of someone who'd already memorized the phrase.

'Better a snot spoon than a Nazi,' Vita replied.

As the men cursed on, albeit in more muffled tones, Orinti said he'd stay and guard them while the others went for help.

'Not on your own, you won't,' insisted Enzo. 'I'll stay with you.'

Vita said she knew the way back to the boat.

'Rosa's coming with me, please,' she said. 'Just in case—'

'Of Giant Sloths?' Enzo asked.

Rosa gave him one of her looks. 'Just because we haven't found one yet, doesn't mean they're not real.'

'We did find a monster, didn't we, like you said before

in the cave,' Enzo replied, giving the canvas a satisfied kick. 'Two of them, actually.'

It was a relief to be back in the forest. The smell was of damp earth and greenness, and something sharp and orangey that Vita said was a type of lily that only opened at night. At first, as they walked, Rosa felt as if her legs weren't quite obeying. They were travelling downhill and, in the starlight, soon found the path they'd made earlier when they were tracking the Giant Sloth. Already, it felt like a lifetime ago. All they'd been scared of then was meeting a savage-clawed beast that may or may not still exist. But the world now seemed more complicated. It was people who did the most damage, not animals.

But she couldn't yet start to think about Herr Eisenhoff, not properly. That was too overwhelming, like walking down a corridor full of doors and not knowing which ones to open. Already, her head was full. And, as the immediate drama of the day began to recede a little, she became suddenly, horribly tired.

'Food,' Vita decided, because she was slowing up too.

They found berries and bananas, and kept walking as they ate. A short time later, the path began to widen. Rosa guessed they weren't too far from the canoe.

'Shame we didn't see a Giant Sloth,' she said as they walked side by side.

'We'll come back one day. I bet it's here, somewhere,' Vita replied.

Rosa glanced around at the dark trees. At night, the forest was an even stranger place, so alive with shrieking animals and singing insects you couldn't see. She felt it then, a prickle at the back of her neck.

'Do sloths ever follow people?' she wondered.

'You'd have to ask Orinti – he's the one who knows all the stories.' Vita glanced at her. 'Why? You don't think we're being followed, do you?'

As quick as the neck prickle had come, it was gone again.

'Sorry, I'm just a bit jumpy – that's all.'

At least Mr Carter wouldn't be bothering them again.

'Was he right, d'you think, about Yara being an agent?' asked Rosa.

'Mr Carter? I dunno.' Vita pushed aside a branch. 'I'm dying to know what my sister *has* been up to. She certainly convinced me she was after the sloth.'

'Me too.'

There was so much Rosa had believed about Yara. That night at Westwood, when she'd shown her around the library, and located Bernard Taverner's actual notebook! And upstairs, later, hadn't Yara perched on the end of her bed, advising her what to pack? She'd looked after her when she was sick on the boat, made sure Vita treated her kindly. None of it felt like a pretence, even now.

Yet there were things that had never added up. Yara on the boat, not leaving the cabin: was she really working, or hiding? Only when they left Portugal behind and the possibility of anyone else boarding the ship, did she unplait her hair, change her clothes and relax. Why did she leave Mr Taverner's notebook at the museum? And her passport, the document that would identify her if anything happened in the jungle? Did she know, even then, the risk she was taking?

It was all so confusing. But Yara had always been a mystery. On the way to Westwood Halt station that day, Rosa was already convinced she was someone else before she'd even arrived.

Orinti's blue boat was where they'd left it. In order to push it out onto the river, they had to disturb a family of capybaras, who were sleeping up against the hull.

'Sorry!' Rosa couldn't help saying.

The capybaras grunted before settling back down on the sand.

On board the boat, Vita sat front left, Rosa rear right. Though it was just the two of them this time, they were travelling downstream, with the current in their favour. They paddled quietly, steadily. The sight of Vita's straight, strong back reassured Rosa. Every now and again she'd still glance at the riverbank. There wasn't anyone there – she knew that – but the *feeling* at the back of her head where her plaits parted, kept returning.

She was tired again too. Above them, the sky was clear, moonless, full of sherbet-coloured stars. The starlight on the river, the soothing stir of water beneath their paddles, made Rosa's eyes grow heavy. Once or twice her chin dropped to her chest. She'd startle awake, paddle with a bit more effort, until her head began to nod again.

'Mind if we talk, so I can stay awake?' she called to Vita, eventually.

'Sure. What about?'

'Tell me about Yara, what it was like when she wasn't here.'

'Okay.' Vita settled herself, pleased to be asked about her beloved sister.

First, she explained about Yara going away to college, how she'd been clever, just like their parents, but, unlike them, had wanted to sit exams and get qualifications, and then to travel the world.

'She was always coming and going,' Vita admitted.

But the war was the longest she'd ever been away.

'We wrote her letters, and she'd reply, but then they stopped. She missed our birthdays and coming to stay with the Xanti, which we do every year. Then our old family friend died, Professor Glastonberry who ran the museum, and she didn't make his funeral.'

Vita paused to stare down at the water.

'Our whole family was different without Yara. I can't explain it. Sure, I had Enzo, and what people say about twins is true enough, but I've got a special bond with Yara as well.'

Though Vita couldn't see her, Rosa nodded in earnest.

'What's your sister like?' Vita asked.

'Oh!' The question took Rosa by surprise.

'She's older than you, right?' coaxed Vita.

Rosa nodded again. 'She was seventeen when I left, so

she'll be a proper grown-up by now.'

'She might be married with a family. You might be an auntie.'

Rosa giggled nervously. 'Gosh, I hadn't thought of that!'

'Was she a nice sister? Are you like her?'

'She looked after me a lot when my parents were working. She wore these green woollen stockings.' Rosa paused as more came back to her. 'And she'd sit me on her lap while she did her homework, and didn't mind when I scribbled on her schoolbooks.'

'She sounds lovely.'

Rosa's nose tingled. Her eyes welled up. Liesel *was* lovely. Remembering it made her even more sad. It wouldn't be so bad if her sister had been a chump, but to miss out on a whole life with someone as wonderful as Liesel felt such a terrible, *terrible* waste.

Vita stopped paddling. 'There must be some way of finding out what happened to your family.'

'People have tried,' Rosa replied. She'd overheard Yara saying as much that night she ran off into the forest.

'Then we keep trying,' Vita said, and started paddling again.

The Xanti heard them coming. By the time they reached the channel where Orinti moored his boat, the bank was heaving with people, all crowding around with lights, talking at once and wondering what had brought the children here in the middle of the night.

'We need Yara's help! It's an emergency!' Vita cried, scrambling out of the boat.

It was Finn who rushed forward, grabbing her by the elbows.

'What's happened? Where's Enzo?' he demanded.

'And Orinti?' asked a woman who seemed to be his mother. 'He went with you, didn't he?'

'Yes.'

'You went looking for a Giant Sloth, didn't you?' she guessed. 'He's talked of nothing else since you arrived.'

'It wasn't a Giant Sloth. It was a Nazi,' Vita said.

A sea of baffled faces stared back at them.

'A *Nazi*?' Maia was the first to speak.

'Yes,' Rosa tried to explain. 'We wanted to help Yara, so we went off to find the beast, but instead we found a man. The Giant Sloth was just—'

'A code name.' The crowd parted a little to let Yara through. Someone put a blanket across her shoulders as she moved stiffly towards them. 'You've rumbled me, I'm afraid.'

'So it is true?' Vita stared at her sister. 'You *are* an agent?'

But the questions had to wait.

'You have to send help to the caves,' Rosa said urgently. 'That's where you'll find Enzo and Orinti. They're guarding a Nazi called Herr Eisenhoff and Mr Carter.'

'Carter?' Finn spat. 'I knew that lizard was part of this.'

Orinti's mother – her name was Jayan – had already boarded the boat. Maia was at the stern, pushing it back into the stream. Once it was in the water, she also climbed in.

'We know the way to the caves; we'll find them,' Jayan promised.

'Go! Go!' shouted Finn.

'Please be careful,' Vita begged them. 'They're not very nice men.'

As Maia and Jayan disappeared downstream in the boat, Yara turned back towards the huts. 'I'll radio for help from the authorities. They'll send someone to meet you there.'

Rosa stared at her: it still hadn't quite sunk in.

'Don't look at me like that,' Yara said briskly. 'It's only a little radio. And no, it wasn't in the backpack you helped yourselves to. I took precautions, just in case you pulled a stunt like this.'

Chapter Twenty-five

Only when the call was made, did Yara finally explode.

'I can't believe what you did!' she cried.

She told them they were reckless, stupid, getting involved in something they didn't understand, and how if it had all gone wrong she'd have had to take the blame. Rosa listened, cheeks burning, holding Vita's hand. They had taken risks. They had done a very dangerous thing. But Yara was wrong about them not understanding.

'I know what the Nazis did,' Rosa said, looking directly at her. 'No one would tell me, but now I know.'

At which Yara's face crumpled a little. The telling off over, she squeezed Rosa's shoulder.

'Then maybe you're braver than any of us,' she said.

Since no one could go to bed knowing Enzo and Orinti were still at the caves, Finn made hot drinks with cocoa beans and honey, and they huddled together under blankets to wait. Finn sat by himself, cross-legged on a mat.

'There's room, Dad,' Vita offered, lifting a corner of her blanket.

But he shook his head, saying he wanted to make sure he stayed awake. The night was cool and being tired made Rosa feel the chill more than usual. Nestled in between Yara and Vita, she was glad of their warmth and the soothing rumble of voices as they talked. It wasn't long before Vita was circling the topic of her sister's job.

'This secret work you're doing—' she began.

'Which I'm not allowed talk about,' Yara replied firmly.

Vita shrugged, pretending not to care. 'Oh well. Mr Carter told us stuff, anyway.'

'Oh, *did* he?'

'Yup. He said you were only pretending to be working on the Giant Sloth project, because really this was all about our other grandfather.'

Yara sighed. 'Can't we talk about this in the morning?'

'Oh!' Vita sat up. 'So, you *can* talk about it?'

'Only the bits relating to our family.'

Now Rosa pushed herself up onto her elbows. Finn stopped sorting the seeds he'd been arranging into piles.

'I've always wondered what really happened to the Fieldings,' he admitted.

It all started, so Yara told them in a quiet, cautious voice, when Maia's parents, the Fieldings, met Herr Eisenhoff in Egypt way back in 1908 when there was a real buzz – a craze – for Egyptology.

'This was over a decade before that other Mr

Carter – Howard Carter – found Tutankhamun's tomb,' she explained. 'There were many exciting discoveries, and lots of money and reputations being made.'

Though the Fieldings had only a passing interest in Egyptology, they were keen travellers who loved to soak up a country's history. One evening, drinking cocktails on the deck of a paddle steamer on the Nile, they were introduced to the eminent German historian Herr Amon Eisenhoff. What they didn't realize was that Herr Eisenhoff was in Egypt to smuggle ancient artefacts out of the country to sell on to art dealers and museum traders around the world. He wasn't really an historian: he was a thief. Even then he was pretending to be someone he wasn't. And, knowing this nice, unassuming English couple wouldn't rouse suspicion at customs, he planted his loot in the Fieldings' luggage.

A few days later, the train carrying the Fieldings was involved in an accident just outside Cairo. No one could understand why a train in good working order should crash so catastrophically. All the passengers, including the Fieldings, were killed, making Maia, who was at school in England at the time, an orphan. Their luggage was never found in the wreckage. Years later, when Yara heard the story, she was convinced Herr Eisenhoff had had a hand in the accident. She didn't have any evidence, though, and by now he'd swapped 'history' for the Third Reich. So she waited. And waited.

And when the war was finally over, and Herr Eisenhoff started running, she went after him.

Rosa had been listening with her blankets clutched under her chin.

'Did anyone ever find the stolen artefacts?' she asked. 'Or your grandparents' luggage?'

'No,' Yara admitted. 'Though I've a feeling Herr Eisenhoff will have bigger crimes to answer for when we return him to Europe for trial.'

'He told us he had business in the city,' said Vita. 'Oil business.'

'There was a company name on that letter, wasn't there?' Rosa remembered. 'Petrochemical something or other.'

She wished she'd managed to keep hold of the papers as proof.

'I bet he thinks he can buy the jungle with his dollars,' Vita added.

'Oil, eh?' Finn curled his lip in disgust. 'So this is a man who committed terrible crimes against the Jewish people – and any others who stood in his way – and now he's come here to spread his greed and disease, and destroy our—'

Finn stopped.

He got to his feet, every muscle tense. He was staring in the direction of the forest.

'What is it, Dad?' Vita asked.

He pointed. 'There, by the palm trees.'

They all stood up to look. Rosa couldn't see anything. It was too dark. But, as she kept watching, she noticed a light moving between the trees.

Torchlight.

Someone was there. Within seconds, the light came closer. A swish of parting leaves, feet thudding on dried mud. By the time they could see the man properly – and his distinctive panama hat – he was only a matter of yards away across the grass.

Rosa's heart punched in her chest.

'Isn't that—?' Vita stuttered. 'Wasn't he—?'

'Following us yesterday? Mr Carter's boss? Yes,' Rosa answered, fear in her voice. 'He must have found out what we did. He's come for us.'

Rosa took a step back. This man was dangerous – possibly as dangerous as Herr Eisenhoff. Mr Carter had certainly been scared of him. Before anyone could warn him to stay back, Finn confronted the man.

'Stop right there and tell us who you are!' he ordered, blocking his path. 'You'd better not be here to make trouble!'

The man stopped. He held out a hand in greeting. There was, Rosa was stunned to see, nothing aggressive about him at all. He seemed almost quite embarrassed.

'Dad, please,' Yara said, going to stand beside her father. 'It's all right.'

Seeing her, the man looked very relieved.

'Dr Fielding! Good evening!' he said in a cheery English accent. 'Got your radio message. What brilliant news! Now, which of these brave children do we have to thank for solving Operation Giant Sloth?'

Rosa was still staring, still trying to work out what was going on.

Thankfully, Vita answered the man.

'There are four of us, actually,' she said, with the bold tilt of her chin Rosa had come to love. 'Two are still at the caves, guarding the criminals. But don't worry – we raised the alarm and help is on its way.'

A look passed between the man and Yara.

'Then I'd say you have the situation very much under control,' he agreed. 'Bravo!'

When the man took off his panama hat, it confused Rosa even more. The truth was he did look familiar. Yes, she'd seen him at the Opera House a few days ago, but then he'd been mostly in shadow and, anyway, it wasn't that.

'Weren't you following us in the jungle?' she asked.

'Only slightly,' he admitted. 'It was Carter I was really following. He was sticking to you lot like glue.'

Rosa frowned. 'You're in charge of him, then? You're on his side?'

'No! No!' The man's hands flew up in distress. 'I work for Dr Fielding – Yara – she's the one in charge of this operation.'

'We work together, really,' Yara corrected him. 'When we realized what connections Mr Carter had made in prison, we knew, if we got him involved, paid him enough, he'd eventually make the mistakes that would lead us to Eisenhoff.'

'So you *tricked* Mr Carter?'

The man rubbed his jaw sheepishly. 'We enabled him to make a mess of things, yes.'

It was a lot to take in. Rosa felt exhausted, and was glad when Yara gestured for them to return to the hut and sit outside again. As they settled onto the collection of logs, mats, blankets, something was whispered to Finn and he set about making more of the cocoa drink.

'It'll help with the shock,' Rosa heard him say.

Things got a bit odd when Yara took her hand. Then the man in the panama hat said, 'I've something important to tell you, Rosa,' and her stomach dropped.

'H-how do you know my name?' she stuttered.

'I'm Leo Swetmund,' the man said very slowly, as if it should mean something.

'Swetmund . . . Swetmund,' she mumbled, testing it out. No, she didn't know anyone with that name.

'I've worked with Yara on this case – and on others – but my main work since the war has been tracking down missing people who –' he hesitated, swallowing – 'were removed from their homes by the Nazis.'

Rosa noticed he was nervous too. Her fingers found an end of plait. Before she could chew it, though, the words were out of her mouth.

'Have you found my mother and Liesel?'

Leo Swetmund pressed his hand to his chest.

'I am trying, please believe me,' he said, seeing the hope in Rosa's face. 'That's partly why Yara brought you here, so I could meet you for myself.'

Rosa stared at him. At Yara. Was this true? She hadn't thought Yara could surprise her any more.

'The Portuguese dictionary on the boat,' Yara reminded

her gently. 'D'you remember I told you it belonged to a friend?'

Rosa thought, gave a small nod. So this man was *Leo S.*

'Your sponsor,' Mr Swetmund explained, 'the family who were meant to take you in when you arrived in England, changed your name to Sweetman to make it sound more English.'

'Oh crikey, I get it,' whispered Vita, who'd been quiet until now.

The frustration was too much.

'Well, I don't, and I wish someone would tell me!' Rosa cried.

Mr Swetmund glanced down at the hat perched on his knees, then up at her. That look, it *was* familiar.

'Rosa,' Yara squeezed her hand. 'This man, this friend of mine, is your father's brother, your uncle.'

For a while, Rosa stayed silent. When she'd imagined finding her family again it was always her mother and sister who'd scoop her up in a hug and cry with happiness. She'd not even been two years old when her father fled Vienna. She had no memory of him, and hadn't known he had a brother.

Now she had an uncle.

It was all too much. Rosa covered her face with her hands.

'I'm sorry,' she said, and started to cry.

The next morning, feeling stronger, Rosa tried again.

'Please don't think you've got a cry-baby for a niece,'

she told her uncle as they ate mangoes at breakfast. 'I'm not normally like that.'

'And please don't think I'm the sort of person who pushes people into orchestra pits,' he replied.

Rosa felt herself going red. 'You saw me? In the Opera House?'

'I saw your feet, sticking out from under the curtain. I didn't know who you were then, but –' he glanced at her English shoes, that lay abandoned outside the hut – 'I've not seen any other children here wearing shoes like that.'

'Lucky them,' admitted Rosa.

'So,' said her uncle with a sigh.

'So,' she replied.

They smiled shyly at each other and agreed to share another mango.

For the rest of breakfast, Rosa couldn't stop wondering. Did Uncle Leo look like her father? Did he have Liesel's ears? The way he tapped his index finger against his cheek when he was listening – was that a family trait? When Uncle Leo finally caught her staring, she had to ask.

'Your father was the handsome one,' he told her, with a fond smile.

Was.

She'd known it all along. But still there was a moment where sadness filled her chest, and her nose tingled on its tip.

'Did he die because of the war?' Rosa wanted to know.

'The *threat* of war made him leave Vienna,' her uncle replied. 'But you were meant to join him in America. He was going to send for you all once he was settled.'

'Why didn't he?'

Uncle Leo took a deep breath. 'First day in New York he looked the wrong way crossing the street. The truck killed him instantly.'

'Oh.' Rosa blinked. 'Oh.'

She hadn't quite been ready for such a sudden, brutal ending. All that hope, all that possibility, gone in a split second.

It was only later, once she'd dried her tears and washed her face and hummed a few bars of her mother's song, that she felt grateful. Her family, for so long, had been a mist in her memory. Finally, from it, the shapes were beginning to emerge.

When the blue boat returned, Enzo and Orinti were so tired their mothers had to help them out on to the bank. Both boys were grinning from ear to ear. It was such a relief to have them back safely, and to hear that Yara's radio call had summoned other agents to the scene. Herr Eisenhoff and Mr Carter were duly arrested and handcuffed, and, at first light, marched through the forest to a waiting boat.

'It was a long old night,' Enzo confessed, yawning. 'So, please, no more adventures for the time being.'

'Hmmm,' Orinti replied. He still had a glint in his eye.

After food and a rest, the boys were dying to meet Rosa's uncle. Like her, they couldn't stop staring at the poor man.

'You've definitely got his big feet,' Enzo whispered.

Vita elbowed him.

'Distinguished-looking,' was Orinti's reaction.

Rosa smiled. 'I like that.'

They also discovered that Uncle Leo liked playing football.

'Fancy a kick about?' he asked them, rolling up his shirtsleeves.

'What with?' said Rosa.

'Aha!' Orinti ran off and came back moments later with a dried gourd. It was smaller than a football, and lighter, but when they kicked it, it didn't fall apart.

Once they'd decided on the best place for the pitch and stuck spears in the ground for goalposts, they spent the afternoon shouting and yelling and running about. It was impossibly hot, and they made up the rules as they went along. Though the twins were quite competitive with each other, Rosa didn't give a fig whose team won. All that mattered were her three exceptional friends and her long-lost uncle, laughing like idiots in the sun.

Meanwhile, the criminals were taken straight to Manaus jail. Once the paperwork was arranged, Herr Eisenhoff would be sent back to Europe, where he'd stand trial for the crimes he'd committed during the war. Rosa noticed how people still took great care not to speak about these crimes in front of her.

One day, not long after their reunion, she asked her uncle to explain.

'In all honesty, I can't,' he said, his face ashen. 'Things were bad enough when your father and I left Vienna.'

'Because you're Jewish?'

He grimaced. 'Yes, though we were hardly what you'd call observant: people didn't have to be. The Nazis went after them anyway. That's why, after your father's plans fell through, your mother was determined to get you to safety.'

Rosa's heart gave a painful twist. This was the most anyone had told her.

'And did they leave, Mum and Liesel?'

'I hope so.' Her uncle shut his eyes, briefly. 'The terrible thing is that we're the lucky ones, we survived – but look what the war's taken from us.'

There was much else Rosa wanted to ask him. But it was impossible to fit seven years of questions into just a few days. At least she knew, for certain, that someone was looking for her mother and Liesel – properly looking – for two people, surname *Swetmund.*

She'd waited this long, she told herself. She simply had to be patient.

Chapter Twenty-six

Over the following days, the weather began to change. Less rain, more fiercely hot sunshine heralded the start of the dry season, which meant it was time for the Xanti to move deeper into the jungle. With so much of the land already cleared of forest, food was getting harder to find, the xaman told them. Bearing this – and everything else that had happened – in mind, Maia and Finn decided to return to Renascida with the children.

'They don't trust us to go back there on our own,' was Vita's take on their decision.

If true, then the children weren't the only ones being reined in. As they were clearing their hut, Rosa overheard Maia warning Finn.

'No spears, no hot tempers. We *talk* to the cattle ranchers, yes?'

'I'll try,' he replied, not very convincingly.

'Good. Because we all want to live together, Finn. It's important we find a peaceful way.'

Just to be certain, while Finn was busy carrying their

things down to the boat, Maia gave his spear to Jayan for safekeeping.

Since Uncle Leo's plans were 'loose', as he put it, he too was coming back to the bungalow for now. Rosa was glad; she didn't think she could face saying goodbye to him just yet. But there was one farewell she couldn't avoid, and she was dreading it.

Deliberately, she waited until almost the last minute when everything was packed onto their boat. She told herself not to cry, not to make a fuss. When she held out her hand to shake Orinti's, he stared at it, confused.

'We're friends,' he insisted. 'We don't say goodbye.'

'But I'm going back to England, soon. I don't suppose I'll ever see you again.'

'You will.' He sounded surprisingly confident of the fact. 'One day you'll come back and we'll find the Mapinguary.'

She sighed. 'Isn't it just a story, though?'

'*Just* a story?' He looked surprised. 'Rosa, our stories are important. It's who we are, who we want to be. It's like music, you know? It helps us find a way when we're lost.'

'Like in the cave?'

'Exactly. And a story, like music, is always alive, always ready to be shared, so there's no need to say goodbye to something that's always there.'

Rosa thought of her mother, scribbling the song on the back of her identity card. And when she started to cry they were good, happy tears.

*

Back at Renascida, Minty was full of the latest news from Manaus. Mr Carter's involvement in the case of a wanted Nazi war criminal was all over the newspapers. He was, somewhat predictably, Minty said, protesting his innocence. Yet not one person of the law had come forward to represent his case in court. The only voice in his defence was the mother of a boy he'd rescued from drowning at Manaus docks.

'*"Surely the man has some good in him?"*' Minty read out loud from the letters page of the *Manaus Morning Herald*.

The incident was still relatively fresh in Rosa's mind. Given what she knew of Mr Carter now, it *had* been a confusing moment. The poor little sailor boy was definitely in trouble. She'd been about to jump in after him herself.

'Mr Carter's an opportunist,' Yara told her. 'If it had suited his situation better to leave the child to drown, believe me, he'd have done that, instead.'

Even Maia, who Rosa had never heard speak ill of anyone, agreed. 'When he took me in as an orphan, his own niece, it wasn't out of any kindness.'

'Money,' Minty agreed. 'It was always the money.'

'It didn't matter in the end, did it?' Maia gazed at Minty, at Finn. It was obvious who her true family were.

Until now, no one had mentioned the inevitable. But, a few days later, when Yara began packing again, Rosa knew the time had come to return to England. Herr Eisenhoff's passage to Europe was booked, and Yara was to accompany him to Lisbon, where he'd be handed over to the authorities for trial.

There'd been a moment when Rosa hoped Uncle Leo might take care of her now. But he'd been called back to New York on a matter of urgent business, and had left Brazil even before they would. So, as had always been the plan, Rosa would be returning to Westwood.

Still, it was a jolt when she caught sight of a return ticket with her name on it, on the veranda table, next to Yara's.

I feel like I'm dying, she thought, then told herself not to be dramatic.

Westwood wasn't all dull: there was Mr Jarvis and the library, and Billy living in the next town. But when Yara appeared with her plain blue skirt and jacket over her arm, checking them in the sunlight to see if they needed cleaning, it all became too real. They were going back to England, in English clothes. Rosa didn't think she could bear wearing tweed ever again.

She couldn't explain it to Yara without sounding ungrateful. This trip had never been forever; that was made very clear from the start. She was lucky – beyond lucky – to have had this opportunity. Back in England, she could write to the twins, and maybe come here again, one day. She just needed to get used to the idea, that was all, and remember what Orinti had said about goodbyes.

'I'm going down to the river,' she told Yara, so she didn't have to look at the blue skirt and jacket any more.

Rosa had it in mind to sit at the end of the jetty and dangle her feet over the water. But, when she arrived, Finn was already there.

Not wanting to disturb him, she tried tiptoeing away. But he beckoned her to come and sit beside him. Even more of a surprise was when he asked about Westwood.

'I've been there,' he said. 'So if you're dreading going back I understand.'

'You do?'

Finn nodded. 'Minty said once, *"Come out, Finn Taverner, and be a man,"* and I've never forgotten it. I don't suppose Clovis has, either. Sometimes you can't keep running away.'

Rosa disagreed. She'd happily keep running away if it meant staying here.

'Why *are* you and Sir Clovis both called Finn Taverner?' she asked.

Finn rubbed a hand over his face. He looked suddenly rather tired.

'It's a very long story,' he said, but told her a shorter version, of the complicated arrangement in which, many years ago, he, Maia, Minty, Professor Glastonberry and Clovis had all played their parts.

'You swapped lives? Wow!' Rosa was fascinated, amazed.

'I couldn't leave here – I'd die if I had to – and Clovis didn't want to stay. It sounds very dramatic, but it made sense to us.'

'Weren't you running away?'

'From the place that's in my heart, my bones? No, never. The Xanti are my family. The forest is my home. Always will be.'

'And Westwood?'

'Over the years, I've tried to forget it ever existed.' Finn smiled grimly. 'But Yara's been pestering me for days now. Clovis needs money. He's after my signature so he can sell Westwood's land to a developer.'

'Who'll do what with it?' Rosa asked, warily.

'Build. I've seen the plans: there'll be main roads, shops, an office block. I can't let Westwood's fields and ancient woodland disappear under all that concrete.'

'Gosh!' Rosa saw the problem.

'You know how I feel about land being sold off.' He gestured towards the forest. 'It's been so terrible here, with the oil company and the cattle ranchers. We've lost so much of our world already.'

Rosa swung her feet, thinking. She understood Finn's concern. But he'd also made Sir Clovis sound as greedy as the ranchers, and that wasn't quite fair.

'You know you could try talking to Sir Clovis, rather than getting Minty to answer his letters,' Rosa said, carefully.

'Our agreement was that he'd never bother me about Westwood again.'

'It's just . . .' Rosa frowned. 'I've been writing to someone I thought was a friend. It's horrid when they don't reply.'

'I'm not agreeing to ruining the countryside. He can forget it.'

'I don't think he sees it like that. He's worried about the house, mostly,' Rosa said. 'It's falling apart. I don't like living there, but that's only because it's not my home. Sir Clovis and Lady Prue were always kind to me.'

Finn said nothing.

'And not just me. They took in lots of children in the war when their homes got bombed,' Rosa continued. 'And the animals from the local zoo.'

Finn stared at her. 'Zoo animals? How did *that* work?'

'Not always very well,' Rosa admitted. 'But it was better than a cage at the zoo.'

They both fell silent, swinging their feet, gazing over the water.

'Tell Clovis . . .' said Finn eventually, 'tell him I'll agree to him selling what he needs, on one condition: that the land continues to be used for animals.'

'What sort of animals?' Rosa asked, to be clear.

'That,' Finn said with a smile, 'is entirely up to him.'

Later that day, they played another hot, noisy football game. Rosa missed Uncle Leo being there, but it was still fun. The teams were bigger this time, comprising Duerte, Josue, all his siblings and the dog Julius, who was brilliant in goal. Work on clearing the forest had slowed considerably, at least on the stretch between the neighbours' houses and the bright new road. Duerte said something to Finn that culminated in smiles and arms being thrown round shoulders.

'What are they so happy about?' Enzo asked, wiping sweat from his eyes.

Vita, who was closer, heard bits of what was said.

'Something about a petroleum company not wanting the land any more. A key investor pulled out. Got called back to Europe, apparently.'

'That's good news, isn't it?' Rosa asked.

The twins agreed it wasn't bad.

'It's a small victory in a colossal war,' Vita said. 'Though there'll be other cattle ranchers, other oil companies, trust me. It's not over yet, not by a mile.'

'Small battles *do* win wars,' Minty pointed out.

'Sometimes,' Maia agreed sadly. 'But I fear for the future, for the Xanti and all the people who live in the forest.'

Rosa remembered how Orinti had called Herr Eisenhoff 'Mr Nazi Oil Man' and couldn't quite share Minty's cautious hope. When someone stamped all over your world and swept it aside as if it was nothing, when your life and all the richness in it – your beliefs, your family, your food, your home, your songs, everything in fact that you valued – was treated like dirt, well, Vita was right: that *was* colossal. And it was, very definitely, something to fear.

Now, it was dusk, and it was Rosa's last evening at Renascida. Tomorrow, she and Yara would be boarding the *Hilary* for Europe, though she didn't want to think about that yet. They were all on the veranda. Maia and the twins lazed in hammocks, Minty was reading, Finn stirring something green into the pot of chicken and beans cooking on the fire. Rosa was sitting very still, watching moths flitting around the lanterns. Just a few weeks ago, she'd come here on a sort of holiday to see the rainforest. She was looking forward to meeting the twins and hopefully glimpsing a jaguar, which she'd write and tell Billy all about, even if he didn't reply. These things had happened. All of them. And so much more.

On quiet feet, Yara came to sit beside her.

'Are you okay about leaving?' she asked.

'It hurts,' Rosa admitted.

'You'll come back one day.'

Which was what Orinti had said.

'Would you mind,' Rosa found herself saying, suddenly. 'What I mean is, is it all right if we – Uncle Leo and I – could be part of your family too? It's just, there are so many of you, and only us two, and you've been so good to . . .' She trailed off, seeing Vita no longer dozing, looking surprised.

'I don't know, Rosa,' said Enzo, trying – and failing – to frown. 'It's not as if we really *like* you, or anything.'

He laughed, then reached out to hug her very tightly and said he could never have enough sisters. Vita started to cry.

'Keep in touch,' Maia insisted.

'A bit of news from Westwood wouldn't hurt,' agreed Finn.

'I do believe that's decided, then,' Minty said, and took out a hankie, insisting she'd something in her eye.

Rosa looked at them, her new, wonderful, fascinating family, and her smile stretched as wide as a river.

Chapter Twenty-seven

The letter arrived in a very roundabout way. It had been posted in New York, sent to an office in London, where it went to Rosa's original sponsor in St Albans, before being forwarded to Lady Prue at Westwood, who then sent it POSTA RESTANTE to Manaus. On the envelope was the name: *Miss Rosa Swetmund*, crossed out with *Sweetman? Sweetland?* and *Not known at this address* written next to it. If the postmarks were correct, then the letter's journey had taken an astonishing two years to reach Rosa. Actually, two years and an hour and a half, because Rosa didn't collect it from the post office herself: that was Enzo, who'd gone to the library, and said he'd check for any post as he went by.

It happened the day they were due to sail back to Europe. All the way to Manaus, Rosa had been a knot of nerves. It wasn't just saying goodbye to the twins and everybody else that worried her. The thought of seeing Herr Eisenhoff again made her throat feel tight, as if his fork was still pressing against it.

'You won't see him,' Vita assured her. 'Yara says he'll be locked in a prison van without any windows.'

Before sailing anywhere, Yara needed to collect her passport from Luella at the museum. Since they'd arrived early at the docks, and Rosa and the twins agreed they'd like to see the Giant Sloth skeleton again, they went with her. To their surprise, the museum was relatively busy when they arrived. The front door was propped open, and a woman wearing big yellow beads, who'd definitely not been here last time, was issuing tickets from a table in the hallway. From inside the first big room came the echoey high-pitched chatter of children's voices – lots of them, by the sound of things. It was this that made Enzo change his mind.

'Ugh! School trip! Bet it's St Joseph's – they always come here,' he groaned.

Vita pulled a face. 'That's Dad's old school, the worst in Manaus. No wonder he only lasted there a day.'

Personally, Rosa had seen enough of Finn to bet any school – good or bad – wouldn't have suited him as a child. But when Enzo said he'd rather go to the town library to look for books on football they agreed to meet at the quayside in an hour.

'I'll be passing the post office. I'll check for mail,' Enzo promised.

'Please, if you could. And ask for *Sweetman* and *Swetmund*,' said Rosa, though once inside the museum didn't give it another thought. By then she was preoccupied with Vita who, realizing she was about her lose her best friend and beloved sister, started to get teary and grumpy.

While Yara went to find Luella, Rosa steered Vita towards the Giant Sloth.

It was here most of the schoolchildren were congregating, a sea of red blazers pointing excitedly and talking very fast all at once. No wonder their poor teacher looked as if she had a headache.

'Is it still out there?' A boy wanted to know. 'Is it a real beast, like Bigfoot?'

He was asking Yara, who'd appeared again with Luella.

Over the top of the children's heads, Yara shared the briefest look with Rosa.

'No one really knows,' she said, a mysterious gleam in her eye.

The boy didn't seem to think much of this answer, but Rosa thought it perfect.

Tipping her head back, she stared up at the creature's enormous skull. She was almost glad they hadn't managed to see the real thing. It would've been totally, utterly terrifying. What they'd found instead was something even more monstrous: Operation Giant Sloth had been a particularly apt name. Rosa wondered what the next mission would be called, because there were more criminals like Herr Eisenhoff out there, and Yara and Uncle Leo were working hard to close down the ratlines and find them. As for the Mapinguary, she prayed with every fibre of her being that it *did* exist, that some force, some spirit of the forest, would protect it from those bent on destroying it.

Mr B. Taverner's notebook, meanwhile, was to stay at the museum. It felt right, Yara said, to keep her grandfather's collection together. She also asked Luella if she had any use for three antique eyeballs.

'Apparently they once belonged to a famous actress,' Vita told her.

To which Luella laughed. 'A three-eyed actress? Now that I'd pay good money to see!'

Midday, and the quayside was hot and heaving with people. Their ship had arrived in dock and was currently disgorging its passengers down the gangplank. Clearly there'd been some changes since the little sailor boy incident, because now uniformed stewards were helping people down the plank, taking luggage, holding uncertain hands, calling out, 'Mind the step!' Among them, Rosa spotted their 'beef tea' steward, helping two women who were struggling to carry an old travelling trunk that was as big as a piece of furniture.

'They'll be letting you on soon, I expect,' said Minty, who was watching everything with a cool, calm gaze.

This waiting was the worse bit. Rosa could feel her nose tingling. She wrung her hands, jiggled her legs, wishing they could just go so this awful dead time would be over. Vita was the same, fidgety and sullen.

Enzo, meanwhile, was late.

'He's taking his time,' Vita muttered, scanning the crowds for any sign of him.

'I hope he makes it,' fretted Rosa.

A drab grey van pulled up at the far end of the quay. From the way Rosa's heart sped up, she guessed it was the prison van with Herr Eisenhoff inside.

'Oh, where *is* Enzo?' Vita wailed. 'You can't leave before he gets here!'

From the prison van, two burly guards emerged. Two more men in dark suits, European-looking, stepped out of another car that had pulled up alongside the van. Their job, so Yara told them, was to guard Herr Eisenhoff's cabin night and day during the journey.

It was then Vita caught sight of Enzo hurrying towards them, red-faced and excited.

'At last!' she said, beaming with relief. 'A snail would've been faster!'

Enzo was beaming too, though not at his sister. Above his head he was waving what appeared to be a very tatty letter.

'It's for you!' he cried. 'Rosa! It's from England!'

'For me?' But, as she reached for the letter, someone else was calling her name. Someone behind her, in the crowd.

Confused, she turned to see a huge, dark wood trunk on the cobbles. And two women, one standing at either end of it, wearing lipstick and powder and looking stunned by the heat. They were staring at her. *Really* staring. Something tightened in her chest. It wasn't the heat that astounded them, she realized, it was the sight of her.

She knew them too. Her mother was thinner, yes, but

still the same tall woman with wavy brown hair. It was Liesel who'd changed the most. Like Vita had said, she'd become a woman, taller than her mother, even.

A sob broke from Rosa's throat. She'd been waiting seven years for this moment, and now it'd come she didn't know what to do.

Her mother came towards her, holding out her arms.

'Oh, Rosie, Rosie, Rosie,' she sobbed. She was the only person who'd ever called her that. Lady Prue tried once, but not again.

Rosa ducked under her arm, pressing her cheek against her mother's blouse. She breathed deeply: thank goodness, her mother still smelled the same – lavender soap and warm skin. Briefly, she pulled back just to look at her.

'It is you, isn't it?' Rosa whispered. 'I'm not dreaming this?'

Her mother kissed the top of her head. 'No, my darling, it's really me.'

But Rosa was almost too scared to stop looking in case she vanished.

Liesel, who had been trying to drag the trunk single-handed, gave up to rush over and throw her arms round what was still available of her sister. She pulled away only for a moment to gaze adoringly at her.

'Look at you, baby sister,' Liesel sighed. 'You're all grown up!'

'Not as grown as you,' Rosa replied.

Liesel laughed and hugged her again. Rosa was glad to

be held so tightly: her legs didn't feel strong enough on their own. Then came another pair of arms. More smiles, more tears, and Uncle Leo was there too.

'I found them,' he cried. 'In New York. A few years too late, but I found them.'

At some point, in amongst the dizzy joy of it all, Rosa had the briefest thought about Herr Eisenhoff. If he noticed them on his way to the ship, he'd see four people standing on the cobbles, clinging to each other with happiness. She hoped he'd realize then, finally, that he wasn't on the winning side.

In the end, the only goodbyes said were to Yara. She had to go to Europe to deliver Herr Eisenhoff to justice, but there was no need for Rosa to go back to Westwood. Why would she when everyone she loved was here?

It was obvious, almost immediately, that Renascida wasn't big enough for two families. Liesel, who had an American fiancé now, and worked as a magazine editor, was due back in New York in a few weeks' time.

'It's where we've been living,' her mother explained. 'We've got a small apartment near the Brooklyn Bridge. It's nice enough. You'd be amazed – the city is full of people like us.'

What she meant was Jewish people who'd fled Europe – Germans, Poles, Austrians, Italians. There were food shops and flower stalls and bars playing late-night music that sometimes made it feel almost like home.

'But we didn't have you, Rosie,' her mother sighed,

touching her cheek. 'Or your father.'

They'd tried to come to England, she said, but crossing the Channel became too risky. America, she said, had let them in just in time. The letter, which Enzo waited patiently until later to give her, was proof that they'd been trying to find her for a long time. As well as the confusion over names, there was no record of Rosa going to Westwood. The list still had her down as living in St Albans, though her original sponsor had since moved away. The only positive was that in hunting for Rosa they'd found Uncle Leo. And the rest was down to him.

Though Rosa had never seen Brooklyn Bridge and thought she'd like to, she didn't feel ready to leave Brazil just yet. Since Liesel was old enough to fend for herself in the city, her mother declared that if Rosa was staying then so was she.

'No more searching for you,' her mother promised.

'No more waiting to be found,' Rosa agreed.

The house they moved into was in the old part of Manaus. Personally, Rosa would've liked something closer to Renascida, preferably on stilts by the river, where she could spend her days watching for jaguar and caiman. But, still, the house was beautiful in the way she'd once imagined Yara's home would be – a tiled courtyard, cool, quiet rooms. It was convenient for her mother who, on hearing the opera house was reopening, started to teach singing in their spare downstairs room.

Uncle Leo came to stay often. Rosa liked him more

and more, and when he admitted he was considering moving to Manaus for good she threw her arms round his neck and nearly choked him.

Weekends were always spent at Renascida with the twins. They were already planning to see Orinti again, if the Xanti agreed, and maybe – if they were brave enough – another trip into Mapinguary country. Their hunger to find the Giant Sloth hadn't died.

Then, on a day when Minty had one of her terrible headaches, the old governess decided it was time to retire. Much to their disgust, the twins were enrolled at St Joseph's in Manaus. It really wasn't a terrible school. Rosa knew – she'd been going there herself these past months and was already almost fluent in Brazilian-Portuguese.

'We can sit with you, can't we?' Vita asked, uncharacteristically nervous on their first day.

'It's already arranged,' Rosa assured her. She remembered all too well what it felt like not to belong, and was proud to be the one now making sure Vita and Enzo felt at home right from the start.

Another letter came from England, a few months later. It sat in a tray in the post office for a week or more, mostly because its addressee, a Miss Rosa Sweetman (now Swetmund, though the sender didn't know this), was too busy and too happy to keep checking her mail.

She collected it one afternoon on the way home from school.

'Just a minute!' she shouted to the twins, who were

269

rushing ahead, as always, to buy cheese dumplings from their favourite street seller.

The letter was from Billy. It was only one side of paper long and she read it quickly. His father, the news was, had struck a deal with Sir Clovis. Back in their new quarters at the zoo, the animals hadn't settled at all. They were pining, his father was certain of it, for the country air. Takings at the zoo were down. More and more people looked to leave the city for a daytrip out. It was likely, if things didn't pick up, that they'd have to close.

After receiving some news from a long-lost friend in Brazil, Sir Clovis had come to them with a proposal. To compensate for the loss of Opal, he'd offer them first refusal on a substantial swathe of land.

The long and the short of it was this: in a month's time, Westwood would open to the public as a wildlife park. There'd be ostriches, meerkats, zebras and, if the circus was serious about retiring their lions, a few of those to lie under the trees.

Rosa folded the letter, thinking. It still wasn't how animals were meant to live. But, since these ones were probably born in captivity, it seemed like a fair solution. And though she struggled to imagine Lady Prue checking tickets or serving ice creams it might well make enough money to mend Westwood's roof.

Billy had also sent her a cutting from the local paper.

'THE BEAST OF WESTWOOD MOOR' the headline said, and below it an excitable account of how locals had reported seeing a large black cat living wild on the moors. No one knew how long the animal had been up there. The grainy black-and-white photo didn't prove much, though the big-cat expert who'd studied it claimed it was a mature female jaguar, looking very fit and well. One rumour was it had escaped from a private collector, another that it had once been part of the zoo that lived at Westwood during the war. Up on the moor, it was flourishing, apparently. At the end of the piece, local chauffeur Mr Jarvis was quoted as saying: 'Ruddy good luck to the creature, that's what I say. Perhaps now she'll get a bit of peace.'

Rosa said a silent thank-you to Billy, who knew she'd love this story. And to kind friends and escaping and being found again. Taking the hot cheese dumplings Enzo was offering her, she linked arms with Vita, and together they walked home.

Acknowledgements

Being asked to write this story was the stuff of authors' dreams. Firstly, I must thank my indomitable agent Jodie Hodges for sealing the deal. You are the wisest. Also Lucy Pearse, who initially was to be my editor, and with whom I had many happy, squealy-with-excitement conversations about Eva, her work, and how a sequel might look. Thank you for choosing me. To Sarah Hughes, who picked up the reins, and was an absolute joy of an editor to work with. Thanks so much for your calm, clear, clever advice and for allowing my story to breathe. And to Thais at Sage and Salt Books in Brasil, whose sensitivity read of the manuscript gave me much to consider – a huge and humble thank you to you for sharing your insights.

Katie Hickey's beautiful illustrations suit the story perfectly – it's such an honour to have your artwork in and on my book. Thanks ever so! And to all at Team Macmillan Children's – Amy B, Charlie C, and the others I've yet to meet, thank you so much for everything you've done to make this story happen. Special thanks to Clare Hall-Craggs, publicist extraordinaire. I cannot wait to get cracking on our schedule!

I'm hugely indebted to Eva's family for trusting me to write a sequel to *Journey to the River Sea*. Thank you seems barely enough. And to my own family and friends who've had to put up with my wistful musings on the Amazon, while the rest of the world was in lockdown – sorry about that.

To fellow authors, publishing folk, journalists, bloggers, booksellers, librarians, teachers, school support staff and all the booklovers out there who've supported me as an author, and shown real excitement for this book, thank you. You are the best.

And finally, to Eva. My heart is full. None of this would've been possible without you.

About the Author

Once told by poet Ted Hughes her writing was 'dangerous', it took Emma Carroll twenty years of English teaching and a life-changing cancer diagnosis to feel brave enough to give her dream of being an author a try.

Nowadays, she's a bestselling author and the 'Queen of Historical Fiction' (BookTrust). She has been nominated for and the winner of numerous national, regional and schools awards – including the Books Are My Bag Readers' Award, Branford Boase, CILIP Carnegie Medal, Young Quills, Teach Primary and the Waterstones Book Prize. Emma is one of very few authors to have been Waterstones Book of the Month twice.

Emma's home is in the Somerset hills with her husband and two terriers. She still can't believe her luck that she gets to write dangerous books for a living.

About Eva Ibbotson

Eva Ibbotson was born in Vienna, but, when the Nazis came to power, her family fled to England and she was sent to boarding school. She became a writer while bringing up her four children, and her bestselling novels, including *The Secret of Platform 13*, *The Star of Kazan* and *The Dragonfly Pool* have been published around the world.

Journey to the River Sea won the Nestlé Gold Medal and was shortlisted for the Carnegie Medal, the Whitbread Children's Book of the Year (now the Costa) and the Guardian Children's Fiction Prize.

Eva died peacefully in October 2010 at the age of eighty-five.